About the author

Tony Andrews is a tall English author and singer-songwriter. He was born in Finsbury Park, North London, and he loves going to the beach with his dog.

LOUISE AND THE LAUNDRETTE LADY

Tony Andrews

LOUISE AND THE LAUNDRETTE LADY

Vanguard Press

A CIP catalogue record for this title is
available from the British Library.

ISBN 978 1 784658 95 3

*Vanguard Press is an imprint of
Pegasus Elliot MacKenzie Publishers Ltd.*
www.pegasuspublishers.com

First Published in 2020

**Vanguard Press
Sheraton House Castle Park
Cambridge England**

Printed & Bound in Great Britain

Dedication

I dedicate this book to all the dreamers out there.
Please keep going after your dream.
Do what makes you happy.
Best Wishes
Tony Andrews

Dear Reader,

I would like to wish you a beautiful, happy, long life filled with love, peace, and laughter…
May the rest of your days be the best of your days… and may you have great friends to share them with.
Tony Andrews

WWW.TONYANDREWSMUSIC.COM

Illustrations by Mark Elmer

Meet The Gang

Betty

Louise

Penelope Jones

Kelly Ann

Max Redwood

Sonic Sasha

Roaring Meg

The Fuzz Cats

Leon

Tigerlips

It's crazy times for Louise when a
Laundrette Lady takes her into another world,
where many dangerous events
and eccentric characters await her.
In this world, a whiskey-drinking witch
has very dark plans for this innocent little girl.
Join Louise in her adventures, and see how
TEAMWORK MAKES THE DREAMWORK!

CHAPTER 1
HELLO, MY NAME IS LOUISE

Hello, my name is Louise Buttersky. I am ten years old, and I would like to share my story with you. Lots of strange things have happened to me in my life, and I want to tell you about all of them. I've been on some wild adventures and I must say, I've had my fair share of crazy moments. Let me start by sharing my very first memory with you: I was three and a half years old, sitting in the back seat of Dad's car happily gazing out the front windscreen. Mum and Dad had just popped to the shops to get some groceries, well, that's what they said, but when they both jumped back in the car, they each carried a huge laundry bag, and they were terribly happy about something. It was the kind of happiness that groceries alone could not bring; something strange was going on. Dad quickly started the car and sped off down the street. Could you believe it? My cheeky parents had just robbed a bank! Mum and Dad were laughing their heads off. I was too young to fully understand what was going on, but I can clearly remember a rich, strong feeling of happiness in the air, which I thought was nice.

Dad drove a very old car; it was a red Volkswagen Beetle. In some countries, they call that car a bug – ours was rusty and shabby, and the engine sounded like a big old lawnmower.

I loved it.

We got away with the bank job. Dad's plan worked like a dream; a huge convoy of old Volkswagen Beetles drove through London that morning. They were on their way to a classic car show in Brighton, a big Beetle gathering, so we just tagged along with them. There were over a thousand Beetles on the motorway; this made it easy-peasy for us to blend in and hide from the police.

Now, a pretty bizarre thing happened to me on the way down to Brighton. It was a little bit spooky but very fantastic. A small red-chested robin, wearing a tiny aviator hat, flew alongside our car as we bombed it down the highway; he kept us company all along the M23. I remember this vividly like it was yesterday. The robin kept looking and winking at me. He tipped his little hat and waved at me through the window. He looked so funny – that cheeky robin gave me the giggles for ten minutes.

"What's so funny, Louise?" asked my mum. I immediately pointed to the robin, but every time she turned to have a look, he ducked down out of sight; he was crafty. For a long time, I thought that robin was just a little character in my imagination, but it turns out I really did see him. He is now one of my friends; I will tell you more about him later.

As soon as we got to Brighton, we checked in to The Grand Hotel, which is located right on the sea-front. My goodness, what a lovely place; very posh and uppity I must say. We stayed there for two relaxing weeks; it was great, and the weather was tip-top. I remember the morning Dad treated me to a nice little watch from the hotel gift shop; it has a little shooting star on its face. I love it so much. I still have it today, but it's all worn out now. I'll always remember what Dad said when he gave me that watch.

"Never forget who you are, my little sweetheart.

You're a magnificent shooting star." He then placed the watch on my wrist and gave me a little kiss, then he tickled me senseless until I cried out with laughter. Dad always knew how to make me smile.

Before heading back to London, my folks decided to buy a new car. We ended up purchasing a small, green Mini Cooper. The Beetle had to go; it was an obvious connection to the bank job. It sounds silly, but I was emotionally attached to that car. I'll get a nice Beetle for myself one day when I'm a bit older.

Heading back to London in the green Mini was a snug journey; my safety chair was squashed in-between two large red suitcases. I was blissfully happy because I had Lemon (my favourite teddy) on my lap and my new watch on my wrist. I had absolutely no idea how to tell the time; I just loved looking at the shooting star on its face. Mum and Dad were blissfully happy too because both the suitcases were completely filled up with cash. We were rich! YES!

About a month after the robbery, my dad decided to buy a nice little cottage in Devon. He picked a small quiet town by the seaside. Dad wanted to get away from London because fish and chips taste nicer by the sea. So off we went to Devon; it was like going on a holiday that we never came back from. Happy days.

Our new cottage was tiny, but the back garden was massive. We had a large black and white patio that looked just like a giant chessboard, and there were hundreds of wild flowers growing everywhere – nice colourful ones, not ugly weeds, and at the very back of the garden stood a gigantic oak tree, with its own rustic treehouse, a great place to read and draw.

We were just two streets away from the beach. I could get out of bed in the morning and have my feet in the sand in less than five minutes if I ran.

My eccentric dad was really into his fish and chips, so much so that after living in Devon for a couple of months, he decided to open his own fish and chips restaurant, right on the seafront; he became a fish and chipologist. Dad also decided to get a swimming pool dug out in the backyard, which was great at first, but after a few months, he started using it as a storage tank for all his fish, which is a bit strange. He's a bit of an oddball, my old man. He loves a good swim, and so does Mum, but she refuses to use the pool now because it's too stinky; Dad still swims in it, with or without fish, crazy fool.

Now, back when I was five, I had a pretty peculiar accident in that pool. My cousin Reggie accidentally pushed me in; fortunately, there were no fish in it at the time. This accident happened in the middle of an intense snowball fight, on a cold December morning.

Reggie's plan was to get me in a headlock and quickly slip a freezing cold snowball down the back of my coat. He ran at me like a wild bull, but the silly sod couldn't slow down in time. Sliding on the frosty grass

Reggie bashed into me like a bowling ball whacking the last pin down. I flew up into the air and landed headfirst in the freezing cold pool.

When I smashed through the ice, it felt like I was being transported into another world – sweet jumping jelly beans, it was freezing cold! Reggie didn't mean to push me in. It was an honest accident, silly twit.

Can you imagine standing at the top of Mount Everest in just your knickers? Or trying to sleep naked in a meat freezer? Well, that's how cold I felt in that pool. My body went into a state of complete shock. I immediately slipped into a trance and sank straight to the bottom. I was down there for about two hours, I think I may have died for a little while.

Reggie lives in Wales now but, just the other day, we had a telephone conversation all about the 'swimming pool accident'. This is what Reg said:

"Louise, I remember everything. I was looking at you in the water, and you were long gone. I waited and waited for you to pop your head back up, but you didn't move at all. You just laid at the bottom of that stinky pool, like a boxer who had been knocked out.

"I was petrified. My heart sped up like a fox being chased by a thousand bloodhounds. I constantly whispered your name as I fought against my fears. I would have shouted your name at the top of my voice, but my throat had closed up; I was paralysed with fear. I thought about jumping in to save you, but I chickened out, so I went looking for your parents instead, but I couldn't find them anywhere. I guess they were both working at the fish and chip shop.

"I really thought you were on your way to heaven, Louise, and that's when something very unexpected happened. A mysterious figure came flying down from the sky, riding on a black surfboard and, with no hesitation at all, the figure dived in and saved you; it was a super-fast rescue. The unusual thing about this spooky sky-surfer was their appearance. It wasn't a person – it was just THE SHADOW of a person. That's right – a dark shadow and nothing else. I didn't give this too much thought because you were being saved, and that was all that mattered to me, but looking back, the circumstances were very extraordinary.

"The shadow seemed angry and hostile. It pulled you out of the water and threw you to the ground like an old rag doll. I was quite nervous, so I ran and hid behind some overgrown rose bushes, and watched the rest of the rescue from there.

"Like a magician, I watched the shadow produce a handful of bright sparkly dust from nothing. The dust was all glittery, like crushed diamonds, and you were still completely out of it, away with the fairies lying on the frosty grass, with your face tilted up to the sky. I knew you were still alive 'cos I saw clouds of mist blow out from your nostrils; you looked totally wasted.

"Holding my breath, I silently watched the shadow

pick you up and rub the sparkly dust all over your head. Your eyes suddenly opened, and a drunk squiggly smile covered your whole face; you looked like a stupid clown, drunk on cider.

"Once the shadow finished shampooing you, it immediately threw you back to the ground and quickly zoomed off. SHOOOOOOOOOM! Just like that, then you suddenly woke up coughing, and soon after that, you puked up lots of swimming pool water."

Yep, that's how Reggie saw it. I believe this really happened because that sparkly shampoo dust changed me forever; it turned my brown hair blue and made it extra thick. I know it was magic dust because I can now store oxygen inside my blue hair and breathe underwater for hours. It's weird, but I like it. It's pretty cool, I guess, but when I need a haircut, it can be a real nightmare; my thick blue hair always breaks the hairdresser's scissors.

"Mamma mia, it's-a like-a tryin' to cut-a through barbed wire!" one Italian hairdresser said.

It got to the point where they banned me from the hair salon. These days, whenever I need a trim, I just use a big pair of garden shears; I tie my hair back and chop the ponytail off. One big snip, and it's all done.

So, who was this super freak on the surfboard? Why did he, or she, save me? Will I ever get to thank him or her? Will I ever get to meet them? Yes, I will because more crazy stuff happens to me a little further down the road; keep reading and all shall be revealed.

CHAPTER 2
FLYING HIGH

A few calm years went by without any spooky stuff going on, but when I reached the age of eight, something 'cuckoo' happened to me in the summertime. I was on the beach with Mum and Dad when I saw this strange man down the far end of the bay. He was looking after some hot air balloons; they were real big mamas. He had a sign that said 'HOT AIR BALLOON RIDES, £10 PER PERSON'. Dad always wanted to go up in a hot air balloon, and he wanted me to come along for the ride, but I wasn't having any of it. I didn't want to be stuck in the sky, sitting in one of those little baskets. I guess that kind of thing just isn't my cup of tea. I'd rather be surfing the waves on my boogie board and secretly breathing underwater with my blue hair; I love doing that.

So, Mum got dragged into it instead.

"We won't be long," said my dad. He wore black sunglasses and red swimming trunks. He would have looked quite cool, only his big beer belly made him look eight months pregnant. In his mind, he thought he was someone like James Bond or Indiana Jones, but he looked more like Humpty Dumpty. My dad made me laugh; his ego was too big.

Mum was a lot cooler than Dad. She wore just an orange bikini with a white T-shirt; she looked good in anything. She's always been a head-turner.

I kept a casual eye on my folks as they lazily walked off down the beach, then I watched Dad pay the old man, and soon after that, they were up in the sky drifting over the bay. I immediately knew something was up because I had this dark uninvited feeling in my tummy, and it wouldn't go away. Every time I looked up at my folks, I kept having to squint my eyes, so I quickly put my sunglasses on, and that's when I realised something strange was going on. It looked as though Mum and Dad were being pulled up to the top of the sky by some kind of invisible force.

"Where are you going?" I shouted. "Come back down!" I pleaded. They couldn't hear a word I said – they were far too far away, then they disappeared!

Sweet mercy, this truly was a sad and heavy day for me, and it affected me in the most awful way. I was absolutely heartbroken. My first reaction was to look over to the balloon man and blame him, but he was already gone; it was like he magically disappeared.

Something sneaky was going on here all right. That was the last time I saw my parents; I was absolutely gutted! I mean, really gutted! It felt like my heart got sliced into four pieces, like a pizza, and two slices got immediately snatched away, right under my nose. I like pizza.

I went back home and cried in bed for two weeks. I was so upset and so lonely; loneliness sucks.

As more weeks passed, I slowly built my strength back up and gradually found the will to carry on living. The toughest part of all this was having to grow up fast, which was no fun at all, but I had no choice. I had to quickly learn how to take care of myself. I carried on going to school. I did all the ironing, all the shopping, all the gardening, all the washing, all the cooking. I fed the rabbits and the goldfish; I even paid the bills. Dad's fish and chip shop closed down; that was a sad day. It was a good thing we still had lots of cash stored away from the bank job. I kept it hidden under the floorboards in my bedroom.

The worst part of all this was the horrible feeling of being alone all the time. I kept in touch with my cousin, Reggie, but that was just every once in a while, on the telephone.

I needed someone to be with every day, someone to come home to, someone to play with, someone to talk to; I felt so lost. I missed Mum and Dad so much. It was impossible for me to hold my tears back; for months and months, I cried myself to sleep every night.

CHAPTER 3
A BLESSING IN DISGUISE

Two difficult years went by, and I was now approaching my tenth birthday, which is on the tenth of March, but on the sixth of March, I got caught up in an unexpected domestic pickle. It all happened on a Sunday night, in the kitchen. I was standing by the sink washing some dishes when the washing machine blew up. Boom! The explosion made such a loud bang. I jumped an inch off the ground, while bits of metal flew everywhere. It felt like a bomb had gone off. The washing machine door flew across the kitchen like a wild killer-Frisbee. It clipped my ear as it swished past my head, then it smashed through the kitchen window and knocked the neighbour's cat off the garden fence.

I quickly fetched my dad's wheelbarrow from the garage and filled it up with broken washing machine parts, then I picked up all my half-washed soggy school clothes and dumped them in the sink, then I mopped up.

This incident was a huge inconvenience for me. I needed my uniform washed and ready for school the next day. I had to act fast, so I quickly stuffed all my heavy wet clothes into a big sack and made a trip into town. There was only one laundrette I could think of, the one on the seafront.

Our town was a lovely town in the summertime. The beach was always overflowing with families and holidaymakers, lots of people slowly cooking their skin under the sun, just lazing about soaking up the mellow vibes.

Some folks even had their own little beach huts. They'd be slumped in their deck chairs, reading books and magazines, licking ice creams, drinking tea, and munching on cakes. They seemed to spend the whole summer just chatting away with family, slowly getting fatter. Lots of grandmothers, parents, and kids; lots of little dogs and lots of old men with big fat bellies.

Everyone always had fish and chips for dinner; I say this because Dad's shop was always busy. But that world seemed a million miles away now. Outside, it was dark, wet, cold, and grey – typical English weather, I guess.

Two minutes after leaving the cottage, I found myself struggling to carry the heavy sack full of my waterlogged school clothes, so I nipped back to get Dad's wheelbarrow. I quickly tipped all the broken washing machine parts out and filled it up with my heavy wet soggies.

I looked awfully silly walking down the street pushing a wheelbarrow in the rain, but I didn't care. I quickly got out to the seafront and noticed how bleak everything looked. It was like being in a ghost town. Nobody was around, and I mean nobody, then I suddenly saw the laundrette over yonder. It was the very last shop on a parade of about twenty shops.

I walked past the sweet shop, the toy shop, the beach shop, the toffee shop, the American Diner, the souvenir shop, the tea shop, the swimming suit shop, the Italian restaurant, the pet shop, the fudge shop, the biscuit shop, the ice cream shop (my favourite), the chemist, the bakery, the Indian restaurant, the English cafe, the candyfloss shop, the cake shop, the international coffee shop, the milkshake shop, and the local dentist – all closed; only the laundrette was open for business.

I'll never forget my first visit to this laundrette; it changed my life forever. Now, as far as laundrettes go, this place was pretty cool. Looking through the window, I could see it was very well looked after. Everything looked pristine, shiny, and squeaky clean; it was spotless. As I approached the front door, I suddenly noticed a rare and exotic flower in the window. It had a big sign beneath it saying: ONE OF A KIND DRAGON-FIRE DAFFODIL FOR SALE (PERFECT FOR HEATING THE HOUSE UP).

That sounded a bit bonkers to me – I guess it was a tropical-flower, it looked exactly like fire that wasn't moving. As I walked in, I immediately felt the heat oozing out from this one of a kind daffodil. It was like walking into a desert; the place was steaming hot.

I quickly took my coat off and swung the front door right back, making sure it stayed wide open. The cold night air swiftly blew in and helped cool the place down. Nobody was about, so I did as I pleased.

Leaving Dad's wheelbarrow outside; I quickly stuffed my clothes into one of the ultra-clean washing machines and immediately put some powder and coins in at the top. I pushed the start button, released a big sigh, stepped back, and parked my bum on one of the pink plastic chairs. I started to relax while I watched my clothes spin around and around. I still felt very sad about my folks; my heart felt heavy and burdened. I guess you could say I had a serious case of the blues.

Then a big gust of wind suddenly blew in. It must have been travelling over the ocean at two hundred miles per hour because it almost knocked me off my seat. I caught a big lungful of the fresh sea breeze; ahhhhh, it was so nice. I took several more deep breaths, then I had this strange feeling come over me like something mischievous was lurking in the atmosphere. It was the kind of wobbly sensation one feels just before an electric thunderstorm kicks off, then I got distracted. All my attention suddenly got drawn to the sound of a beautiful singing voice coming from outside the shop. Its volume grew louder and louder, and that's when I saw her – this pretty woman walked in looking like a cosmic pop star. She was stunningly beautiful – it was the laundrette lady. She looked so bright and lovely; anyone could tell that she was a positive soul.

Her energy was pure joy and happiness, and her personality came across as fizzy and carefree. Maybe she was a Sagittarius, or a Pisces perhaps? She came into the laundrette holding a mop and bucket. She was using the mop as a prop; it was her 'pretend' microphone. I think in her imagination she was performing a huge ballad at the Hollywood Bowl. Her unique voice gave me goosebumps; she was super talented. She blasted all her feelings right out from the pit of her tummy. I was completely moved by her big spirit, but the coolest thing about this woman was the way she seemed to be positive and relaxed about everything.

Let me describe her appearance: the first thing that caught my eye was her big pink fuzzy hair. She had it all fluffed up like candyfloss.

Her eyes glowed like big green traffic lights that said Go-Go-Go. They sparkled behind a large pair of purple framed glasses, and her skin was lovely. She had hundreds of rusty-looking freckles sprinkled down her arms. They looked like tiny tattoos of autumn leaves, and the large freckles looked like cornflakes dipped in honey – her face was so pretty!

She wore blue jeans and a white T-shirt, and over that, she had a big apron on; it had large black and yellow stripes. She was the prettiest Queen Bee I'd ever seen. She had cool flip-flops too; they were purple with giant plastic sunflowers on them, and she smelled like coconut.

She caught my presence in the corner of her eye but continued singing anyway. I found that to be quite a bold move. If I was singing all alone and someone close-by suddenly spotted me, I would have probably stopped and curled up like a shy hedgehog, but not her – she was a song blaster.

This Laundrette Lady filled me with curiosity and intrigue. Who was this wacky woman, and why is she so happy and enthusiastic about everything? I'd like to have some of that energy – it was powerful, magnetic and infectious. It was like she had pure sunlight trapped inside her body, and it had to be sung out.

Five minutes went by, and I continued watching her every move. She sorted out lots of different washes, taking clothes out of the small machines and putting them into the big drying machines, then she folded up all the dry clothes into nice neat piles.

She was entertaining to watch because she blabbered away to herself endlessly. It seemed like every thought that passed through her mind automatically popped out of her mouth. She babbled away about something, then sniggered on about nothing, then there was silence before she giggled out loud; she was lovely. Her zany nature cheered me up, that was for sure, then she finally looked over and said something.

"Hello, Ducky girl, d'ya fancy joining me for a nice hot cuppa tea with a bit of lemon sponge cake on the side?"

How could I refuse?

"Oh yes, please," I said.

"Yippee! Teatime with a stranger." She danced and skipped over to her little hatch and switched the kettle on, then she came over and gently shook my hand as she introduced herself.

"My name is Betty." She smiled boldly.

"Hi Betty, I'm Louise, it's very nice to meet you."

Lovely Betty, I thought to myself.

We sat and talked, drank tea, and ate lemon sponge cake; it was so yummy. It was like being at an indoor picnic, then we got into a very nice conversation about pop stars and tropical flowers.

The sugary icing on the lemon sponge cake gave me a nice little energy boost, then I looked out to the ocean and saw how the weather had changed for the worse. The soft drizzly showers had slowly turned into a wild and crazy thunderstorm; it was practically on top of us. The rain came crashing down like it was its last performance ever, and the wind blew ferociously with no mercy. Betty rushed over to the shop entrance and quickly closed the front door, then my wash finished, so I took my clean clothes out and put them into one of the big tumble dryers. This was the moment I suddenly felt a sadness inside. I felt sombre because it was almost time to head back to the cottage – the empty lonely cottage, where nobody was waiting for me. That place didn't feel like a home anymore; it felt more like a prison.

"What's the matter, lovely?" asked Betty. "Why the sad face?"

I told Betty all about the strange way my parents had disappeared on the beach, and I told her how lonely

I was. I was trying so hard to be brave and strong, but I just couldn't hold my tears back. I felt like a total idiot crying to a stranger, but Betty was compassionate and unjudging. She opened her arms and gave me a little squeeze.

"There, there," she said. She suddenly locked her arms around my waist and got in real close for a big bear hug. I lost my breath for a moment, then she finally backed up and sneezed in my face before making a small announcement. Betty was completely unafraid of eye contact. She looked in my eyes for a good ten seconds; those big green beauties almost hypnotised me. She took a deep breath.

"Louise, I have a little idea. Now, I know this is going to come off sounding a bit nutty, but I'd like to invite you to stay over for the night." She smiled then she spoke some more.

"I do love this beautiful storm with all its glorious thunder and rain, but I really don't want to be sending you home in it. You'll get absolutely drenched to the bone, and you'll probably end up catching a cold, so why don't you stay with me in my cosy apartment upstairs? You can crash in the spare room. Everything always feels better after a good night's sleep. I'll wake you up at six, cook you breakfast and send you on your way." Betty truly was a kind, dotty angel.

I took a good long look outside and felt a cold shiver run right through me. The thunder and lightning sounded like they were having a passionate argument with each other, and the rain fell so hard, so I thought… 'Hot Damn, I'm gonna take a chance.' I turned to Betty and said, "Oh yes, please, Betty. I would love to stay over if that's all right?"

"Yippee!" she said.

"Of course, it's all right."

"I'll go make your bed."

Betty was a true-blue sweetheart.

CHAPTER 4
AN UNEXPECTED WAKE UP CALL

The first thing that caught my eye in Betty's spare room was the huge solid oak bunk bed; it looked so inviting. I quickly climbed up on the top bunk and got ready for bed. The mattress was super soft, and the cotton duvet felt like heaven. The wild storm outside was in full swing now; lots of crazy 'ocean-swish' kept bashing itself against the window. I kind of liked it – it made the whole room feel extra cosy.

I had a good long look around before I switched the light off. It was impossible to ignore Betty's huge pictures. One was a picture of Niagara Falls, another was a picture of the Grand Canyon, and the one by the big window was a huge picture of a Californian Redwood tree with a car driving through it. Some of those trees grow to over one hundred meters tall – far out!

As I examined these pictures, I noticed Betty was in all of them, standing in the corner smiling brightly, with an ironing board tucked under her arm, she looked like a cosmic surfer-girl. I found that to be a bit odd, but I guess Betty is quite an odd and eccentric sort of lady, so I didn't give it too much thought. My intuition told me I was safe in her apartment, and that was all that mattered to me.

It suddenly dawned on me that I was extremely tired, so I quickly switched the light off, said a little prayer and, after ten seconds, I was gone, sound asleep, snoozing away like a relaxed happy bear cub.

I fell into a deep sleep and, after a few hours, I started dreaming about having a delicious Sunday lunch with my folks, but then I suddenly got rudely awakened by a loud aggressive whacking noise. It sounded like racing cars smashing into each other just outside my window; it was terribly disturbing. The bedroom walls shook like jelly.

Bam! Another big wallop. I jumped down from the top bunk and quickly crept into the lower bunk; the blankets were stiff and cold. Boom! Another earth-shaking bazooka-whip. I hopped out from the lower bunk and slid under the mattress. I was petrified now. My goodness, this was a horrible way to be woken up. It was all a bit too crazy for me. Then the bedroom door suddenly burst open, and Betty came rushing in.

"Get dressed, Louise! Nice and quick now – we've got to get out of here, my little darling.

She's only gone and found us. I don't know how, but that's definitely her outside!"

"What are you talking about? What's going on?" I asked. Betty looked right into my eyes.

"Ok, listen. I'll give you the short version now and the long version later. There's a crazy witch outside, and she's come here for you. She wants to get a hold of you – big time baby. There's something you've got, and she wants it!" Betty's voice was deadly serious. I knew she was being honest because icy shivers ran all the way down my back; I kind of liked it. I was scared but, at the same time, I felt alive and full of adrenalin.

"A crazy witch? This is a joke, right?"

"No, it's not a joke. This is real, but I can tell you a joke if you like." Betty giggled a little.

"Why is she after me? What have I done wrong?" Betty took a deep breath.

"I will explain everything later ok, I promise, but right now, we need to stay alive and that means we have got to get our cute little cupcakes out of here, on the double." Betty quickly put some pink ski goggles on and handed a white pair to me.

"Here, put these on!" she said. I did what I was told, then I quickly put my jeans on.

"Oh, lovely," she said. "The white goggles go really well with your sky blue hair."

My goodness, Betty was too much. We had a crazy witch on our doorstep trying to blow us up, and all she could think about was fashion – crazy lady.

I watched her get all worked up with some funny exercise moves, while I put my socks and trainers on. She took short breaths followed by long deep breaths, then she jumped up and down on the spot, performing some rather impressive star jumps; she behaved like a nincompoop fruitcake.

"Come on, baby!" she said. "Come on, baby, who's number one? Betty, that's who." She continued jumping about. "Take me home, daddio. Take me back to the Bing-Bang-Boo!"

What on earth was she going on about? Then she suddenly started moving her hips and waving her arms about in a slow, groovy 'Rub-A-Dub' style. Oh dear, I thought to myself, what have I gotten myself into?

Betty quickly put a bright red puffy ski jacket on and threw a pink one over to me.

"Here, Louise, put this jacket on. It's cold out." I threw it over my arms and quickly zipped it up, then I took a sneaky peek out the window, only to see that there REALLY WAS a crazy witch outside. She was throwing exploding conker bombs at us.

She laughed with an evil rasp of wickedness in her throat. She kept perfect balance on a black flying surfboard that hovered just a few inches above the ground.

Bam! Another exploding conker bomb hit the building, these tiny malicious banger-bombs were making huge cracks in the walls. This was insane; this witch was a first-class psycho. She had these big red eyeballs that sizzled like hot lumps of coal.

Betty pulled me away from the window and quickly

took me downstairs. We hurried past all the washing machines and headed towards a back door which had the words 'Staff only' scribbled on it. Betty karate kicked the door down and dragged me into what looked like a dusty old boiler room. This room had well over a hundred rusty old ironing boards stacked up against all the walls; it looked like an ironing board graveyard. Pushing all the ironing boards to one side, Betty quickly ripped the carpet up, and there was an old wooden trap door sitting right in the middle of the floor. I thought this was our escape route, but I was wrong.

Betty opened the trapdoor and quickly pulled out a massive supersonic ironing board, it was very different from all the other boards. It had a huge rocket-pack attached to its underbelly. She quickly started it up like a lawnmower, then she threw it to the ground, where it hovered and hummed quietly, behaving like a well-trained dog waiting to be told what to do.

"This is my jet-powered rocket ironing board, Louise – it's our safe ticket out of here. It's time for you and me to hit the skies and have some fun with this speed racer. Are you in?" Betty hopped up on the board like a confident pussy cat.

"Absolutely!" I said.

"Ok, move fast, my little angel. Jump on board and wrap your arms around my waist. I'm about to take you on a ride that's gonna blow your brain into another dimension. Just make sure you hold on tight, ok, honey."

Betty suddenly pulled a whistle out of her pocket and blew on it.

"All aboard!" she giggled. I quickly hopped up and threw both my arms around her thin waist.

"Tickets, please," she giggled even louder now.

"Stop being silly," I shouted. "Come on, let's go! Let's get out of here!"

The rocket board suddenly made a huge majestic rumbling noise, sounding like an angry dragster-car getting ready to blast off into outer space.

"Here we go, baby!"

SCHOOOOOOOOOOOOOOM! We blasted out the front entrance of the laundrette like a bullet from a gun. Betty gave that evil witch a good firm slap on the face, just as we swished past her. That really got her riled up; she was properly vexed now.

"You're it!" shouted Betty.

We raced up into the night-time sky like a blazing firework and, before I could blink, we were already flying out over the Atlantic Ocean.

My goodness, that rocket board moved so fast. This was the moment I realised that Betty was a true-blue-wild-hearted-danger-loving-kamikaze-daredevil-waco-kid!

She shouted at the top of her voice, "Never grow up, Louise! There's too much fun to be had!" She's right, you know. She was bold, brave and fearless. A fierce, feisty fire-angel, full of substance, that was Betty through and through.

I took a quick look over my shoulder to see how far ahead we were. Now, the only thing I could see behind us were two red eyes, sitting like brake lights in our slipstream and, when the crazy witch flew closer to us, I saw just how big her eyes actually were. Sweet mercy, they looked like two red hot tennis balls made from volcano lava.

This witch's determination was very intimidating, and her negative energy was like a vacuum trying to suck me in. She was still throwing those awful conker bombs; she had such a nerve.

Both Betty and the witch kept amazing balance as they surfed through the night-time sky. I was scared out of my socks, but the adrenaline was fantastic. We flew past some Canadian geese and shortly after, Betty said, "Hey, Louise. Welcome to your first wild goose chase." Then she laughed out loud like she didn't have a care in the world.

CHAPTER 5
THE CHASE

This crazy chase really was a matter of life and death. The witch followed us like a possessed Terminator – maybe she was the Terminator's grandmother?

I tried to take my mind off the current situation by checking out all the beautiful night-time scenery; the stars above were so pretty, they glimmered in the reflection of the ocean. I guess the heavy thunderstorm from the night before had rolled on down to Spain. It was nice surfing through the evening sky, but it would have been nicer if we weren't in such a hurry. Sky-surfing at top speed on an ironing board is an extremely intense and dangerous sport. I was trying my best not to throw up; I guess the stargazing helped me hold my puke down. Millions of stars silently looked down on us, like pitiful angels.

We flew at ridiculous speeds slashing through the skies like a couple of military missiles. I held on to Betty's waist with all the strength I could muster, then we hit an air pocket and got caught up in some turbulence. The ironing board jumped and jolted all over the place making me lose my balance. My legs suddenly got swooped out from underneath me and started flapping about in the wind, like ribbon-tassels tied to the handlebars on a kid's bike.

I had an obscene amount of adrenaline dancing in my heart, then I felt my grip loosen. My hands were so sweaty, but I somehow managed to keep my little arms wrapped around Betty's waist. I locked both my hands into each other, like two pink spiders hugging – making one big fist – then I finally regained some stability over my legs. I don't know how I did it, but I managed to get both my feet back on the board. After that close shave, I knelt down and squeezed the board with all my might. I felt safer crouching low under Betty's legs.

MElmer 19

Looking just in front of me, I noticed that the ironing board had a mini sat-nav system built in to the digital speedometer. Holy smoke, we were travelling at 1750 mph! Is that possible? This was totally crackers, but it sure was a lot of fun. The power of our speed pulled all the skin on my face right back, and the sound of the roaring wind blew ferociously around my ears; it felt like a hurricane was trying to get inside my brain.

I turned my head to have another quick look behind us, and there she was, still on our tail – those crazy red eyes glowed with rage. This witch meant business; she was so determined to catch us.

Betty was right about the ride. It was, without a doubt, blowing my mind into another dimension.

We soon arrived in America, then I heard Betty's voice in my head, "Next stop, New York City!" That was weird. Betty was somehow able to communicate with me through her thoughts; it was a neat trick.

I looked out in front of us and saw all the buildings of New York City up ahead, then I saw the Statue of Liberty beneath us. We swished past her in half a second.

Betty proceeded to fly straight into downtown Manhattan, weaving in and out of all the high-rise buildings. The red-eyed psycho witch followed close behind us, then I noticed a big green button on the ironing board's control pad. It had two big words printed on it: LONDON FOG. Betty quickly communicated some more thoughts to me.

"Hit the green button, Louise!" That was all I heard, so I quickly reached over and pushed the button down as fast as I could.

What happened next was one of the coolest things that I have ever experienced. The jet-powered rocket board's exhaust pipe spat out huge amounts of thick mist – it was pure London fog – and after thirty seconds, the whole of Manhattan was covered by a huge blob of smoky London smog. It was great, and it made a perfect hiding place. We slipped into the fog cloud and hovered quietly. Soon, everything was super quiet, then the crazy witch followed us in. My goodness, the fog was so thick, I couldn't even see my hand when I held it up in front of me, but I heard something all right – it was the heavy breathing of that psycho witch. Sweet Jaffa Cakes, she was right beside us; we kept completely still.

"Don't breathe!" said Betty, in thought mode. This thought communication technique came in very handy, but it can only be done when the person is right beside you – that's what Betty told me.

I felt the witch's bad vibrations all around us. They were so heavy, and her breath was disgusting; it smelt like fox poo, and she belched constantly. She took short, snorty breaths, sounding like a pug dog having an asthma attack, and the stinky smell of her body was atrocious – oh my goodness – she stunk like the armpit funk from a fat sweaty man sleeping in bed all day scratching his bum, watching TV, and eating cold pizza slices. Sweet heavens above, what a foul repulsive stench; she needed a bath big time.

Everything was intensely quiet and still, then I suddenly felt Betty's arm slip around my waist. She whispered three thought words to me: "Hold tight, honey!" That was all she said, then the jet-powered rocket board suddenly revved up like a wild chainsaw, and we shot out from that foggy cloud like a bat out of hell. We headed straight back to England. This time, the ironing board picked up even more speed; that's when Betty telepathically communicated a thought idea to me.

"Lie down flat on the board, Louise!" she thought to me. "We'll get back to England much faster this way." I did just that, and Betty laid on top of me; this made us more aerodynamic.

Heading back over the Atlantic Ocean, we reached a top speed of 2555 miles per hour. Yeah, baby, I had to 'bear-hug' the ironing board just to keep myself from getting blown off. But my grip wasn't strong enough, the G-force was too powerful and I ended up getting snatched out from under Betty's body. I got swooped out by the lethal wind and was suddenly left behind, I was now free-falling in the middle of the sky way above the Atlantic Ocean, falling fast towards the freezing cold sea below. I saw my whole life flash before me, I was just about to hit the freezing ocean when, SHHHHWIIIINNG! Betty returned, she made an ultra-fast supersonic U turn, and came back just in the nick of time. She snatched me out of the air about two inches above sea-level. Holy Ravioli, that was a close one!

I thought Betty was going to fly slower after that wobbly wipeout, but I was wrong. She got us back up to crazy speeds, but this time she held me extra tight.

We overtook five aeroplanes after that; I heard their engines as we whizzed past them. This whole experience felt like a crazy dream. We were probably travelling close to the speed of light, maybe, I don't know. What I do know is, we got back to Devon super quick, and the crazy old witch was nowhere to be seen, thank goodness.

Betty had tears in her eyes when she saw the state of her seafront laundrette; the witch smashed it up good and proper. It looked like a bomb site now; it was a heartbreaking sight to see. It used to be such a beautiful place. Betty seemed to shrug it off and move on pretty fast.

"We need to get over to the tumble dryers," she whispered.

"Why? Have you got some washing you need to finish?"

"No, silly," she giggled. "I have an escape plan."

"Ah ok," I said, then I suddenly looked down and saw Betty's beautiful dragon-fire daffodil lying pot-less on the floor. I quickly picked it up and handed it to her;

it wasn't so hot now. I think it only gets hot when it's in soil. Looking around, I saw that all the washing machines and all the big tumble dryers were totally smashed up – those lethal conker-bombs were hardcore – then I heard some low, heavy creaking noises. It sounded like the whole building was going to collapse any second.

Betty quickly flew us over to the last tumble dryer right at the back of the laundrette. This dryer had a sticker on it that said, 'OUT OF ORDER'. She ripped the sticker off and opened the big round door, and we gently flew in.

"Hello, what's this all about?" I asked.

"You'll see in a moment," to avoid banging her head Betty crouched over me, then she placed her chin on top of my head.

"Not everything is as it seems, my dear," she said.

"You're telling me," I said.

Betty's voice was a bit more relaxed now. Her calming energy rubbed off on me, and I was pleased to feel it.

We were away from danger, for the time being at least. The tumble dryer looked like a normal dryer from the outside, but once we got inside, there was a secret tunnel which led straight to London.

"We're not safe here in Devon anymore, Louise. I'm going to take you to my West London laundrette; it's a good place to hide out."

"Ok, let's do it," I said. I was enjoying this adventure, and it felt much safer and wiser to keep moving.

I was in no hurry to see that crazy witch again. She seemed to have pure evil energy in her blood – very unpleasant to be around.

Betty started explaining, "I have a secret hideout cave that sits a hundred meters below ground level; it's directly under my West London laundrette. We'll be safe down there, for a while anyway."

"Great. Let's get moving," I said.

So, off to London we went.

After fifteen minutes of tunnel travel, Betty patted me on the back and said, "Watch this." She then pushed a little red button on her Casio calculator watch. It triggered off a 'self-destruct bomb' back at the laundrette. We suddenly heard a deep echo of a huge explosion vibrate through the tunnel; it felt like a mini earthquake. The laundrette back in Devon was well and truly demolished now.

"If you're going to do a job, do it properly!" said Betty, with a little snigger. "Oh well, it was a lovely laundrette, never mind, onwards and upwards, mustn't dwell on the past." Betty's sadness for the loss of her Devon launderette was very fleeting, I must say, I was impressed with how she seemed to shake it off so fast. I reckon she's a Sagittarius, her heart was full of fire.

The good news was this: we had successfully

covered our tracks. The entrance to the secret tunnel was well and truly buried under a pile of steel beams, bricks, and smashed up washing machines now.

Betty spoke up once more, "Louise, I can safely say that we won't be coming back tomorrow to collect your school clothes. Ha ha!"

Betty had a very mischievous laugh, it echoed right down the tunnel. After ten minutes, the echo boomeranged its way back up towards us, and we laughed some more.

It took longer than I thought to get to London, about two hours. Betty flew with great skill and dexterity. She carefully manoeuvred the jet-powered rocket board through all the narrow parts, ducking and diving her way through the long tunnel.

Then, we finally arrived. Yes! Sitting on that jet board for two hours wasn't exactly travelling business class. I was hunched and crouched over for far too long; I felt stiff all over.

It was so nice to finally stand up straight and have a good long stretch.

Betty stretched out too, then she kicked her shoes off, brushed her teeth, and flicked the kettle on.

I was taken aback by Betty's strange collection of weird stuff down in her hideout cave – I will get to that in a minute.

Betty kept herself busy with her dragon-fire daffodil. Stealing some soil from her Chinese evergreen plants, she replanted the daff in a new pot and gave it some water.

"I'll take this lovely flower up to my laundrette tomorrow; it needs sunlight," she said.

Betty looked like she'd just gotten out of bed, her pink bushy hair was more puffier and fluffier than usual, this made me smile; then the kettle boiled. Betty slowly poured herself a nice hot cup of green tea, then she made a nice cold glass of pineapple juice for me, and we plonked ourselves down on the two brown armchairs that sat in the middle of the cave.

At last, we had some time to soak up some peace and quiet.

"You can go back to sleep now, if you like," said Betty, as she laughed out loud. Laughter seemed to be the best remedy for us to shake off all the stress we accumulated from the ordeal we just went through.

Our spirits chilled as we both slowly unwound, then Betty suddenly stood up and said, "I'm going to have a quick shower; I feel stinky. I need to freshen up."

"Sure, ok," I said.

I tried to meditate for ten minutes, but my heart was still beating too fast.

Betty's Laundrette

CHAPTER 6
THE TRUTH WILL SET YOU FREE

It was impossible to sit back and relax because I was too intrigued with Betty's collection of weird stuff, her West London hide-out cave was like a secret emporium filled with freaky things. I decided to have a good long look around while the legendary candy floss-head sung in the shower. Let me tell you what I saw: there were plenty of old witches' broomsticks sitting around, maybe thirty, a very old skateboard made from dinosaur teeth, a pair of turbo-powered roller skates (equipped with mini nitro-rockets), an automatic robotic metal detector with flippers and fins (you could drop it in the ocean and it would come back with gold pieces), there were two pink wetsuits, complete with all the best scuba diving gear and ten ironing boards, all with twin rocket-packs attached to their underbellies.

I saw a huge bookshelf made from dinosaur bones, looking closer I saw a little bowl of marbles sitting on the shelf among all the dusty books; and next to the bowl was a yellow 'post-it-slip' with a scribbly message that said 'Don't lose your Bing-Bang-Boo-marbles Betty!' My O my, what a potty-girl Betty is.

All around the top of the cave were lots of little wooden shelves filled with old broken washing machine parts. Betty also had a funny-looking fridge and a weird-shaped cooker that looked over a hundred years old.

After her shower, Betty came out wearing a green and black stripy dressing gown. She briskly walked over to a small cupboard and pulled out a petrol-powered garden blower; it looked like a hairdryer for giants. She went straight to work on drying her pink fluffy hair.

"Give us a hand, please, love," she said. I was happy to help. Spending time with Betty was quite a unique experience. I pointed the blower right into her face and watched her make all sorts of silly expressions. She was like a perfect eccentric auntie, with a spicy appetite for danger. Once her hair was dried, waxed and styled, Betty threw her jeans back on, found a clean T shirt and sat back in her armchair. I decided to join her and planted myself back in the other one.

"I like your weird-looking fridge and cooker," I said.

"Oh thanks," she said. "I love working on my little projects. About seventy years ago, I found an old Spitfire fighter plane that got shot down in the war. I wanted to keep it so I decided to salvage the metal; that's when I got the idea to turn it into a fridge." Betty opened the fridge door. Inside, there was a loaf of bread, some sausages, and a cheesecake, and at the very back was the Spitfire's propeller spinning gently in a calm fashion. Betty installed it specifically to help keep the fridge extra cool.

"Oh, I must go shopping soon," she said, then she cheekily poked her finger into the cheesecake, scooping a humble sample onto her fingertips, which she immediately licked off. Then she talked some more, "After I finished making the fridge, I saw that I had lots of Spitfire metal left over, so I decided to make a gas cooker as well." She pointed over to the other large shabby piece of metal; it was a vintage gas cooker, and it most certainly looked like the only one of its kind. It was full of dents, it looked battered but it also looked great.

Betty also had a big fat chunky coffee table cut out from an old English oak tree, and on it sat a beautiful Tiffany lamp. The lamp had stained glass dragonflies in its pattern, and when she switched the lamp on, all the dragonflies slowly flapped their wings up and down – hocus-pocus baby.

After seeing all this stuff, I arrived at the foregone conclusion that Betty was batty but in a nice sort of way.

I was feeling pretty zonked out, so I let myself slouch back in the armchair, and by the sound of Betty's sigh, my guess was she felt the same way. I sipped on my pineapple juice while she stuffed a big chunk of tobacco in her old smoking pipe. Her eyes were fixed on me; she had this cheeky smile that kept my eyes fixed on her. I had a burning question that I had to ask.

"Betty, you said you found the Spitfire plane seventy years ago. The thing I don't understand is, you look like you're only twenty-nine years old, so what's the deal?"

Betty's smile suddenly increased, but she was in no hurry to answer me. Moving slowly, she gave her glasses a good wipe with a dark purple handkerchief, she then lit her pipe and started puffing away. She folded her right leg over her left and waited for a long moment before she finally spoke up.

"I have quite a bit of explaining to do, don't I, Louise? Well, let me start by saying that I just love your beautiful blue hair. I think it's absolutely fantastic-bombastic!"

"Oh, thank you," I said.

Betty's tone of voice suddenly changed from relaxed to more up-tempo. "Ok, Louise, make sure you listen up, my love, because I want to tell you everything."

I sat up and nodded an affirmative 'Yes'. My ears were open, and my mind was switched on to full alert. Betty now had my undivided attention.

She began, "Ok, I'm actually over a hundred years old, Louise, but that's not really too important, like most women, I don't like talking about my age so let's skip that subject and get to the more important stuff.'

"I want to tell you about two shooting stars that once cut through the skies at ridiculous speeds. One was called 'Roaring Meg' and the other, 'Sonic Sasha'. Now, these two stars were ultra-fast, swishing from universe to universe at the speed of light, then one dark afternoon up in space, they accidentally crashed and smashed into each other, this happened just when they were passing over planet Earth. Now, this made the biggest explosion ever. Their crash looked like a huge firework exploding in the sky; tons of white glitter sprayed and sprinkled everywhere.

"Now, let me tell you something about shooting stars, Louise. They fly so fast that it takes them about two hours to gradually slow down, so, after the big collision, these two shooting beauties bounced off the moon and started making their way down towards planet Earth, they were still moving at a wild speed. They slashed through the Earth's atmosphere and landed in America, in a state called Arizona. This happened many, many years ago." Betty took a slow confident puff on her pipe.

"Now, when they arrived in Arizona, they hit the ground so hard that they ended up tearing through the solid concrete, ripping through the Earth's surface for miles and miles. Their crash landing created a huge magnificent valley behind them – today it's known as The Grand Canyon."

"Oh, very interesting," I said, then Betty continued.

"The next thing that happened to these two shooting stars was something quite unique; the impact of the crash knocked them out of their socks. They were completely unconscious sleeping under a huge pile of their own shiny stardust, but when they finally came around, there was a big change in their appearance – they had been transformed from star-form to human-form. In simple English, they now had human bodies, bodies with great powers. This was the day Roaring Meg became the first witch ever to exist, and Sonic Sasha became the first wizard ever to exist."

I suddenly laughed out loud.

"I'm sorry, Betty, but that all sounds like a complete load of rubbish. Do you really expect me to believe this crazy story?"

Betty took another puff on her pipe, she then replied with a cool, calm tone in her voice, "Well, you've already met Roaring Meg. She was the dotty witch chasing us over the Atlantic Ocean just a few hours ago. I know this story sounds nuts, but I said I'm going to tell you everything, so please keep listening."

I nodded a sulky yes as Betty continued.

"Now, I will tell you what happened to the stardust. The huge pile of stardust at the bottom of the new canyon shined beautifully under the sun, but it soon lost its sparkle and, as strange as it seems, all the stardust particles slowly turned into little bugs. After maybe half an hour, these little bugs turned into mini witches, and they ended up becoming Roaring Meg's witch army. It was like all the good energy went into Sonic Sasha, and all the bad energy went into Roaring Meg, and Meg passed her bad energy onto the stardust."

Betty had a very simple way of explaining things, which I really appreciated.

She rambled on, "Sonic Sasha was a different story altogether. He knew the witches were going to be a problem, and he wanted to do something about it, as soon as possible."

I was curious now, so I asked, "What did Sonic Sasha do to sort out all the witches, Betty?"

Betty smiled, "Well, being a wizard, he had a very fiery imagination, and he soon came up with an excellent idea."

"What was the idea?" I asked.

"Sonic Sasha flew to the moon and built a beautiful witch library, made from solid marble. He then disguised himself as a witch and persuaded all the mini witches to come up to the library, to learn hundreds of dark evil witch spells.

"The witches agreed and followed Sonic Sasha to the moon, but this was all a trick. As soon as the mini witches were all in the library, a trap door came crashing down, and they were captured. It was never a library; it was a solid marble prison."

I spoke up, "So, Sonic Sasha trapped all the witches in a solid marble prison, up on the moon. Is that what you're telling me?'

"Yes, that's right, my dear. All the witches got

trapped except for Roaring Meg, and for over a million years, Meg has been trying to free her mini witches, but she can't because she's still looking for the only key that will open the prison door."

That's when Betty pointed at me.

"Why are you pointing at me?" I asked.

"Because, YOU ARE THE KEY."

"What do you mean, I am the key?"

I was confused now, so Betty explained things in more detail.

"Well, when Sonic Sasha created the marble prison, he knew it would be too simple to just have a normal key to open the prison gates, so he decided, in his vivid spur-of-the-moment imagination, that only a human boomerang-shaped rib bone would open the main gates."

"Why did he go for that idea?" I asked.

"Because human boomerang-shaped rib bones don't exist – until now that is." Betty pointed at me again.

I felt nervous now. "Are you telling me that I'm the only human in the world who has a boomerang-shaped rib bone?"

"Yes, my darling, that's exactly what I'm saying."

Betty continued, "Roaring Meg knows all about this, Louise. Your funny little rib bone is a very specific shape, it's the perfect size to work as a key, to set her mini witches free. This is what she's been waiting for, and she's been waiting for over a million years, so you must be ready, my love, Meg will be bashing down our door, very soon."

"You must also remember that Roaring Meg is a complete Waco-Nut-Job!"

Betty giggled as she slapped my knee; she was trying to loosen my nerves.

"Louise, there are three things you need to know about Roaring Meg: One, she's ferociously strong. Two, she doesn't have a conscience, and three, she will do absolutely anything to get what she wants."

"You've got to respect her persistence and determination; respecting her strength will help you stay alive."

Betty walked over to the kitchen and flicked the kettle on once more.

"I need a coffee," she said.

I was feeling quite unsettled. I touched my rib cage and, for the first time, I noticed that one of my ribs felt a little bit like a boomerang under my skin. I was in trouble all right. I listened to the kettle boil, then I caught a whiff of the fresh coffee Betty was preparing – it was a nice smell. Betty sat back in her armchair, sipped on her fresh coffee, and immediately burnt her lips.

"Mamma Mia, that's too hot!" She quickly grabbed my pineapple juice and took a big gulp.

"Ah, that's better." Then she suddenly saw how upset I was, so she decided to call for a little timeout.

"Louise, I think it's time for us to have a little cheesecake break."

We stopped chatting and gave all our attention to the cheesecake. It was super yummy; it had a soft crumbly biscuit base with blueberry jam on top. Betty kept her eyes closed while she ate her slice. All was quiet, until she released a huge thunderous burp. Being a lady, she immediately placed her fingertips over her lips.

"Oops-a-daisy, that never happened." she said with

a little wink. I giggled at her as I nibbled on my cheesecake, then the break was suddenly over, and Betty started rambling on again.

"You know, Sonic Sasha the wizard was my father, but he died from a very strong magic overdose in 1973. He pretty much vanished into thin air, and nobody has seen him since." Betty paused for a long moment. That's when I saw a fleeting glimmer of sadness in her eyes. She quickly snapped out of it and talked some more.

"Now, you can understand why Roaring Meg saved you from the swimming pool accident, back when you were just five years old."

"How do you know about that?" I asked.

Betty calmly whispered to me.

"Well, my little darling, some people know a lot about little things, but I know a little about a lot of things." Betty laughed out loud.

"Meg knew about your rib back then, and so did I, but it was best that I kept out of the picture – till now of course. Meg knew she had to wait for your rib to grow; it was too small back then. Meg also understands that this window of opportunity is just for a limited time only. You're still just a child, Louise – as more time goes by, you will naturally keep growing into a young woman, and your boomerang rib will naturally keep growing too. Soon, your rib won't be the right size to open the marble prison door, so get ready, my dear, because Meg will be coming soon, probably sooner than you think. She is one crazy old bat, please remember this, and respect her determination.

"You must also remember – more than anything in this world – that Meg wants to free those witches, she's a sick old girl who wants to take over the whole planet. That crazy witch wants to take over the whole human race, control their minds. Roaring Meg is flipping nuts – you must always remember this!"

I listened to Betty intensely, I felt lucky to have her on my side; she was my guardian angel.

CHAPTER 7
ON THE ROAD AGAIN

I sat back in my armchair and tried my best to digest all the info Betty had told me; it wasn't easy. It's not every day you find out that a crazy witch wants to catch you, rip your chest open, and take one of your ribs away.

I tried to relax, but I couldn't. There was an overflow of energy in my thoughts, and I just couldn't switch it off. Silence filled the cave, but my mind was full of chit-chat. That all changed, however when we suddenly heard a deep rumbling sound come from behind the cave walls. It sounded like a rumble of hunger from a dragon's belly.

"Oh dear, it can't be," said Betty. "Looks like Meg has found us already." I stood up and said,

"Holy crackers with cream! That was quick!"

Betty grabbed my hand and quickly took me into the cave next door. It was pitch black, then we heard a second rumble. Betty sighed as she spoke.

"Oh dear, Meg sure is an angry old girl." Betty slapped the cave walls, making noises like a wild crazy animal.

"Moooooooooooooooo! We're over here, you crazy

old cow!" She didn't give a hoot about Meg, she seemed to be carefree about everything, then she quickly clapped her hands, and a light came on.

"Right, Louise, here's the situation. I've got this other project I've been working on for some time, and due to our present circumstances, I think NOW would be a perfect opportunity for us to give it a test run. What do you say?"

"Absolutely yes!" I said. "I just hope your project gets us out of here, fast!"

"Oh yes, it will certainly do that." There was a relaxed confidence in Betty's voice. It was nice to hear; it gave me some comfort.

We were now standing in front of a large mystery object. It was sitting under an old canvas cover, so without wasting another second, we quickly pulled the cover off together.

"Hello, what have we got here?" I said.

At first glimpse, it looked like an old racing car. It turned out to be a one of a kind, custom-made, sixty-six valve, twin-turbo, low-riding sports car, made completely out of old washing machine parts – it was awesome! Betty built the whole thing from scratch: the wheels were old washing machine drums, the steering wheel was an old washing machine door, the beefy engine was made from ten different washing machine motors – it was ridiculously powerful. The only things that didn't come from a washing machine were the seats. In the front, there were two old sports car bucket seats from an old Porsche, and in the back, was a big old Chesterfield sofa, a tatty red one.

Betty quickly checked the fuel gauge – it was almost empty – so she swiftly opened a big box of washing powder and poured the whole lot in.

"What are you doing?" I asked.

"I need to fill it up," she said. I couldn't believe what I was seeing.

"You mean to tell me this car runs on washing powder?"

"Yes, of course," said Betty.

As soon as the tank was full, we both jumped in and put our seat-belts on, Betty then started rubbing her legs up and down like an excited child just before she was allowed to open her presents on Christmas morning, "Hoooeeee, I'm looking forward to this," she gave me a wink and a smile.

"I call this baby, 'The Spinner'," then she slapped my leg with frivolous happiness. She was terribly excited about giving her unique vehicle a 'make or break' test run; the spinner was a most peculiar invention. Betty started her up on the first try, this made her smile with a glint of pride in her eyes. The engine first sounded like a low humming Harley Davidson motorbike, but after five seconds, it made strange swish-swash popping sounds, it sounded like a dishwasher with a severe case of the hiccups. No smoke came out from the exhaust pipe, just foam, and bubbles.

We suddenly felt the cave walls vibrate again. Meg was close by now. I felt the negative vibrations of her evil witch-rage lurking in the air; it was a dark, morbid yukky feeling.

The spinner suddenly jolted forward a couple of feet, "Hold on to your eggs and apples my little Lou-Lou!" Shouted Betty. She pushed her foot flat down on the accelerator pedal, and the spinner shot-off like a pinball!

"Whooooo-hooooooo! Nice Job, Betty" I shouted.

"Ha-Ha! Let the good times roll baby!" Was her reply.

We drove up a dark winding tunnel that led straight out onto the streets of London. A secret doorway opened, and the spinner came bursting out onto Portobello Road, West London.

We quickly dashed past a Spanish restaurant on Tavistock square. We had to get out of the area fast, but it wasn't going to be easy because the spinner kept slipping and sliding all over the place. The engine was too powerful; it wheelspinned like we had a hundred wild horses trapped under the hood. The sheer speed and power of this vehicle was just too much; Betty kept bashing into things.

I suddenly heard a huge crashing sound come from behind us. I looked around to check things out, and that's when I saw another strange vehicle come up from under the ground. It smashed through the pavement in the most disgraceful way. It was Meg all right. She was driving an advanced high-speed tank, an ugly looking concrete-crusher.

As soon as I saw Meg's red eyes, my body got possessed by a wave of potent fear. I tried my best to turn my nervous feelings into excitement. It wasn't easy; I nearly wet my pants.

Meg followed us all the way up Portobello Road, which is a one-way street, and we were both going the wrong way; the spinner zig-zagged all over the place.

I shouted to all the people on the street, "Move out the way!" People jumped on top of parked cars and into shop doorways to avoid getting crushed. Meg was gaining on us fast; her robust concrete-crusher was surprisingly quick.

As we turned a sharp corner, Betty noticed a couple of fat people sitting at a bus stop. They were both drinking coffee and scoffing jam doughnuts. As fast as a cheetah, Betty stopped the car, ran over, picked them up, and threw them on the Chesterfield sofa in the back. I had no idea what she was up to.

"What are you doing?" I shouted.

"Trust me," she said.

Meg was heading straight for us. She wanted to ram us, but Betty quickly zoomed off – she did nought to sixty in under five seconds – then she turned to the fat couple and spoke up.

"Good morning, sir. Good morning, madam. Unfortunately, there are no buses today, but don't worry, we will take care of you, me and my little sidekick here are happy to give you a free ride to your destination, so please hold onto your knickers and don't fall out!" Betty punched her fist right up in the air and, like a wild cowgirl, she screamed a big 'Yeeeee-Haaaaaaa', like it was party time.

I struggled to hold my laughter in, then I turned and looked at the chubby couple and saw how freaked out they were, the poor souls were in a state of complete shock, but they still managed to carry on eating their doughnuts, while spilling coffee over their laps. They held onto that sofa with all the strength they had. After scoffing his doughnut the fat man quickly put his hands together and started praying, the fat woman squeezed her doughnut so tight that all the strawberry jam squirted out and landed on the fat man's face, I had to quickly put my hand over my face to cover my smiley laughter.

I was impressed with Betty's idea; her quick thinking paid off very well. Our new backseat passengers turned out to be the perfect solution for our car troubles. Their combined body weight held the spinner down beautifully. It stuck to the road like a go-kart now – no more wheelspins or sliding out of control. Meg was still close behind us though; her concrete-crusher ripped through the road like a mad bulldozer, leaving a trail of destruction behind it.

Betty took a few sharp left turns, followed by some razorblade rights, but it seemed impossible to lose Meg; she had a one-track mind. We suddenly smashed through some black iron gates and found ourselves in Hyde Park. The chubby couple in the back were hugging and holding on to each other now.

"Where are the seat-belts?" yelled the big woman.

"There aren't any. You just have to hold on tight, cookie!" shouted Betty. We sped right through Hyde Park like a wild chicken being chased by a crazy fox. Betty was right – Meg is ridiculously determined. We came back out on the main road and zoomed straight past the Royal Albert Hall.

"Oh I say, look at that," said Betty, she was pointing at a huge poster, "The Rolling Stones have a gig coming up. One night only!" Soon after that, we were outside Buckingham Palace. We must have spun around that gold statue, out by the front gates, at least twenty times.

This was the first time I got a clear view of Meg's revolting face. My goodness, she had such strange hair – it was all thorny, like bramble. I couldn't see her eyes all that well, they were hidden behind a big pair of black biker's goggles, but I still saw that red fiery glow shining through. She snarled like a crazy mongoose. She had black horrible pirate teeth with yellow gums, and they suddenly popped out! Yuk, they were dentures. For a second, I thought it was a frog leaping out from her mouth. Meg skillfully caught them and shoved them back in her gob; this really made my stomach churn. Meg truly was a horrible creature. She had lots of bushy nose hairs and warts all over her face, and the long whiskers sprouting from her chin looked like broken violin strings. She also had white strings of saliva drooling down from her mouth. I couldn't imagine anyone ever wanting to give her a kiss.

Betty was getting a great deal of enjoyment from this car chase; she was a genuine adrenaline junkie. She switched the radio on and turned the volume way up.

"Oh, I love this song!" she shouted.

It was 'Free-Bird' by Lynyrd Skynyrd

The old couple in the back were now using their phones to take pictures of Buckingham Palace. Betty looked over her shoulder and spoke up.

"Let's take you around the back, my sweet little darlings. We can get some lovely shots of the royal garden." Betty drove the spinner right through the main gates of Buckingham Palace and sped across the courtyard.

Meg followed as we drove around the west side of the palace. We almost hit a gardener, he dived out of the way just in time – mamma-mia! Crazy Roaring Meg was still hot on our tail, but she was a terrible driver. She bashed into everything like she was driving a bumper car at the fairground. Maybe she was drunk?

She took chunks of concrete out of the palace walls and drove straight through a beautiful garden shed. Both our vehicles made such a mess; we ripped up the back lawn something terrible. Meg drove through six lovely water fountains, and Betty demolished four beautiful marble statues.

The chubby couple in the back were taking as many pictures as possible now; they were acting like the paparazzi.

The next thing that happened took all of us by surprise. Meg reached over to her black surfboard in the backseat of her vehicle and, faster than a wasp, she flew over to the spinner, swooped down, and yanked me right out of my seat. My goodness, she moved so fast!

"Louise!" shouted Betty. I was filled with terror! Meg had a mighty strong grip on me. She locked me under her arm, and squeezed me tight into her body; her hands were like bear claws.

Meg laughed aggressively, as we flew off together on her aerodynamic surfboard. She was one mean old witch.

Her tight grip slowed all the circulation down in my body, making me feel heavy and dizzy. I was so scared. Betty drove back out onto the main road and tried her very best to keep up with us, but it was no use – Meg and I were already flying halfway off into the distance.

"Hang on, Louise! Hang on!" Betty shouted. "Don't give up! I will find you!" I was hunched over, feeling giddy, slipping in and out of consciousness. I just about managed to give Betty a quick thumbs-up, then I felt Meg's surfboard pick up speed as I slipped into unconsciousness. It was like being in the middle of a dark nightmare. I had no idea where she was taking me; it wasn't Disneyland, that was for sure.

Betty quickly made her way back to Portobello Road, dropping the chubby couple off at Ladbroke Grove tube station. Arriving back at the laundrette, she wasted no time at all. She first went down to fetch her jet powered rocket board from the hideout cave, then she knocked back a cold cup of coffee and got ready to leave the premises. Just before she took off, she went back up to the laundrette and placed her dragon-fire daffodil on a small table just inside the shop, by the main window, lots of sun in that spot. Then she blasted off into the sky and came looking for me – go Betty!

CHAPTER 8
THE TOUGHEST DAY OF MY LIFE

Betty's mission was simple: she needed to find me before Meg stole my rib away, but things didn't look good. I was already in Meg's witch cave somewhere on the outskirts of North London. I say 'witch cave', but it was more like an old deserted warehouse.

Betty knew how to find me; it was a 'mind over matter' situation. She flew herself up to a high point in the sky and meditated, while her iron board hovered for a few minutes; her senses were ultra-sharp. Breathing deep and slow, she relaxed herself into a peaceful vibration, and this automatically put her on a higher frequency level. In this relaxed state, Betty was now able to hear my voice. She's a very talented individual, you know; she IS the daughter of a wizard after all, just don't mention her age.

The warehouse in North London was cold and bleak, and I must say, this was without a doubt, the hardest day of my life. This was the day Meg strapped me down to an old wooden table and cut me open.

Don't worry, it didn't kill me; I made it through, didn't I? Of course I did, I'm here telling you my story, but it was still a very rough day, to say the least.

With no remorse whatsoever, Meg ripped my little boomerang-rib straight out from my chest. My goodness, it was so painful. She used a blunt old dagger, and she laughed like a crazy little googly eyed goblin girl while she performed this terrible operation. She didn't behave like a responsible doctor, oh no, she acted more like an obsessed cave woman.

"Yes! Yes! At last! I have the key!" Meg shouted. This was a glorious, victorious moment for her. She held my rib up high and bounced around the warehouse like a super-freak. She behaved like that happy-go-lucky tiger from Winnie the Pooh, she soon started bouncing a little too high, and her head smashed the light bulb above her. Without any warning, she started receiving electric shocks. The hanging light must have had a strong level of electricity passing through it because it held her up there for a good ten seconds. She jittered and wobbled about while all the other lights constantly flickered on and off, then her dentures fell out again, and all the other light bulbs suddenly exploded, that was the moment she fell back down to the floor.

I couldn't see much with the lights off, but I heard a thud, and that was followed by a noise that sounded like a big fart, then I heard some grumpy growling grovelling groans, Meg rolled about on the ground like a wild dog who just got hit by a car. Then I heard a tiny fart followed by small witchy giggle. Meg soon got back up on her feet and started bouncing around again. It was awfully dark in the warehouse now; the weather outside was grey and grim, there was just a dim orange flickering light flashing through the window, it came from an old faulty street lamp outside.

Roaring Meg behaved like she had just won the world cup and wanted to show her trophy (my rib) to the world. In the limited faint light, I saw her knock back a pint glass of Jack Daniels whiskey, she didn't drink it, she just gargled for a few minutes, then she spat all the whiskey back in the glass. Yuk, it looked revolting, the glass now had cockroaches swimming in the whiskey, then she knelt down and picked her dentures up off the floor and dropped them in the whiskey glass, knocking the drowning cockroaches down to the bottom, oh dear.

She then walked over and offered the glass to me, "Fancy a drink, love?" I closed my eyes, turned my face away and nodded a faint no – she was disgusting!

Meg started laughing, dancing and spinning around, then she raised her glass and looked at me with a toothless smile.

"To your rib," she said.

"Bottoms up," she downed all the whiskey with all the cockroaches, and slipped her dentures back in her mouth too, all in one big swooping gulp. This solo toast was followed by a huge belch that echoed all around her old shabby warehouse.

Sweet heavens above, this was the day I realised just how horrible Meg truly is, but I must admit, the stunt with the dentures was a pretty good party trick.

Everything in my mind started to make sense, you know. I finally understood why she saved me from that freezing cold swimming pool, back in Devon, when I was just five. It was all about this moment; it was all about getting her hands on my boomerang rib.

Holy, hot potatoes. I thought this was the end for me. Meg left me lying in a puddle of my own blood. I'm sorry to tell you this; I know it's not a pretty picture, my strength and spirit were on very thin ice. I can honestly say from the bottom of my heart that this was the toughest day of my life.

I watched that crazy gipsy witch put my rib into her mouth and bite down on it hard, she had all the characteristics of a self-centred psycho. She then hopped back up on her black surfboard and flew right out the door. I looked out the window and watched her disappear off into the cloudy sky. It was pretty obvious where she was going – she was off to the moon.

She left me to die on that old wooden table; my heart and soul felt crushed. I was losing blood fast, I knew this to be true because my temperature had dropped right down, I was absolutely freezing.

"Betty," I murmured. I kept whispering her name, time and time again.

"Betty, please find me!" I said this about two

hundred times for the next twenty minutes; I felt so weak.

Then, finally, my prayer was answered. My wild and eccentric surrogate super auntie arrived in the most glorious fashion. Betty smashed through the big window standing like a legend on her jet-powered rocket board; broken glass flew everywhere, yes!

I knew I was dying because I kept seeing this bright white light in front of me. It was an angel coming to collect me, then I heard Betty's bossy voice shout at the angel.

"Go away!" she said. "Louise has her whole life in front of her. Come back another time, when she's ninety-nine years old." The bright light slowly disappeared.

"Hang in there, Louise," shouted Betty.

"Let the rescue commence!" she announced, with a cheeky tone in her voice.

Thank goodness for Betty. She quickly wrapped me up in her big red ski jacket and flew me out of there.

I had no idea where we were heading. Everything in my mind was fuzzy, but I vaguely remember her saying something about going to a cemetery.

"You need purple magic," she said.

Betty did everything she could to keep me alive, bless her soul.

Purple magic is something that lived inside Sonic Sasha's heart. Sonic Sasha used purple magic to create the amazing marble prison on the moon. Purple magic is the opposite of black magic; purple magic is rich and light and full of healing properties.

I never knew this but once a year, every Christmas morning, Betty went to visit her dad's grave in Highgate Cemetery, just to wish him a Merry Christmas.

Well, this was the exact place she took me.

At first, I thought she was going to bury me right next to her dead dad. I had no idea what she was up to. The fire in my heart was dying out; I knew that much. As soon as we landed, Betty immediately started digging.

Her plan was to try and find some of her late father's bones. She believed her dad's wizard bones just might have some purple magic sleeping inside them, deep in the marrow.

Betty was fully aware that her dad disappeared from a magic overdose, and she knew there was only a slim chance of finding something at the graveyard. No coffin was buried at his funeral, but Sonic Sasha was a crafty, shrewd dude. He thought like a fox who knew how to play blackjack and win every time. Knowing her father had a forward-thinking attitude, Betty believed fervently that he may have left something buried at his tombstone, something helpful.

It was late in the morning, and I was dying right there on the cold ground, but Betty wasn't a quitter –no Sir, far from it. She wasn't going to just let me lie back, turn up my toes and kick the bucket – that wasn't her style.

She moved as fast as she could, digging like a crazy jack russell, then I suddenly saw that bright white light come back – oh no, here we go again.

"No!" shouted Betty.

"It's not her time! Go away, angel girl. Louise is staying here with me!" The holy light faded away again.

My goodness, Betty was so bossy.

"Keep strong, Louise!" she said.

She dug awfully fast, but found nothing – no bones, no coffin, not a thing.

My only goal at that time was to keep breathing, but that became more difficult because lots of cold earth kept landing on my face and falling into my mouth, it was making me cough.

Betty was flicking the earth all over the place. She dug like a crazy mole looking for treasure, not thinking about where the loose earth would land, well most of it landed on me, then she suddenly hit something – yes! The sound was like a low-pitched thud. Seconds later, Betty pulled out an old wooden shoebox, excellent!

A warm feeling of hope suddenly filled the air. She quickly opened it and found two items inside: a letter and a rib bone – sweet! The rib had a strong purple glow to it; it must have been one of Sasha's ribs.

"Hold this!" said Betty, placing the rib in my hand. As soon as I touched it, I immediately felt stronger; I knew I was absorbing some sort of unique healing power. Whatever it was, it brought me back, then Betty quickly read the letter.

This is what it said:

'To my darling daughter, Betty.

This is your father, Sasha.

I have some good news, my dear – I'm still alive. I live in a small quiet village in Italy, high up in the mountains. I had a feeling that, one day, someone might be needing one of my ribs, so I decided to leave one in the cemetery. It has a great deal of purple magic inside. It will help the poor soul who needs it, no doubt.

Betty, I love you with all my heart and would love to see you again, please come and visit me soon. I have missed you so much! I will explain many things to you in more detail, when I see you.

With everlasting love,

Your father, Sasha.'

The letter filled Betty up with joy and excitement; she had tears in her sparkly green eyes. She was going to see her dad again – how cool is that? This blew her mind. Betty quickly wiped her tears away and turned all her attention onto me.

"Right!" she said. "Let's get you sorted."

There was a fresh new happiness in her voice.

Betty gently took her father's rib out of my hand and placed it on top of my open wound. She kept still and watched over me like a confident nurse. She took a deep breath as the rib suddenly started to work its magic; it glowed intensely like it was waking up.

I saw this with my own eyes. It gave off a wonderful pinkish/purple light, then it changed to a fiery dark orange. Betty smiled kindly as she patiently watched the marvellous purple magic go to work on me. This magic knew exactly what it was doing; it's an advanced conscious living intelligence.

I watched the rib firmly push itself into my wound, changing its shape as it went in. It hurt like hell, but only at first, then all the pain suddenly disappeared. The rib was brimming with positive energy now. It automatically installed itself into my rib cage, positioning itself perfectly in the vacant spot where the boomerang rib once sat; it moved in forever. It's still in me now, sitting comfortably. I was fixed in sixty seconds. Purple magic is a wondrous thing.

Betty gently placed her hand around the back of my neck and slowly encouraged me to tilt my head up. I slowly got up on my elbows and looked down at my open wound. I watched with wonder as my body speedily knitted new skin over my open chest – it was amazing. I was so impressed. Purple magic seeped deep into my flesh and bones and started circulating its way all around my bloodstream. I could even taste it in my mouth. It was like warm cinnamon mixed with brown sugar and honey; I could get used to this.

Betty was the coolest girl ever. I stood up feeling like a brand new person. I quickly gave Betty a big thank you bear hug; I felt great.

"Thank you, Betty," was all I could say. "Thank you, thank you, thank you so much!"

"Breathe deep, girl," was all Betty said. I suddenly began to really cherish being alive. A feeling of gratitude came right up from my toes, filling my whole body. Betty pulled her father's letter out from her back pocket and showed it to me. I noticed his Italian address scribbled on the back.

"Well spotted," she said. "That must have been quite a traumatic experience for you, Louise."

"Yes, it was a bit wacky," I said.

Betty's eyes suddenly lit up like big green emerald diamonds exposed to sunlight.

"Hey, I have a great idea! Let's go and get a couple of milkshakes!" She smiled like she was ten years old.

"We have no time to waste. I know a good milkshake bar just up the road."

She slapped my bum and jumped up on the rocket board.

"Come on, let's go." So, off we went.

My milkshake had freshly chopped strawberries mixed with vanilla ice cream. Betty's had crushed coconut biscuits mixed with Belgian chocolate ice cream – yummy.

Betty drank her shake way too fast; she was anxious

to get out to Italy. She was ultra-keen to see her Dad again, which is completely understandable.

All these strange happenings were very extraordinary, but deep down inside, I was loving every minute of it.

Betty stood in a power stance with both hands on her hips; she looked like a superhero. Well, she WAS a superhero to me.

"Right!" she said.

"Are you ready to Rock and Roll and Ramble on some more? It's time we head over to Italia!"

I smiled and nodded enthusiastically, while I sucked hard on my milkshake straw.

"Good," she said "Hop back on the board, my little darling." I finished my shake and did just that.

We had to be quick – Roaring Meg was probably on the moon by now, tinkering about with my boomerang rib, slowly figuring out how to open the marble prison.

We quickly zoomed back up into the cold sky and put London behind us.

"Italia, Italia, here we come, baby," shouted Betty.

This was my first trip to Italy, Bella Bella Bella!

CHAPTER 9
LUNCH IN THE MOUNTAINS

The flight to Italy was great. It was breath-taking gliding through all the beautiful Italian mountains; everything looked super fresh and glorious. It also felt good riding on the rocket board with nobody chasing us. I wasn't exactly sure which part of Italy we were in, but it was like being in another world. There were snow-capped mountains everywhere, and all the valleys below had big lakes in them. When the sun hit the surface, they shined shamelessly like huge puddles of liquid silver. The natural beauty of this environment stood out magnificently – the birds singing, the mountain streams, the breeze in the trees. It felt like paradise.

Arriving at Sasha's place, I became super excited to meet him, but I thought it would be best to just play it cool and sit back. I knew this was a big deal for Betty, seeing her dad for the first time in years.

Sasha had his own little business – it was a one-stop roadside-coffee shop, mainly used by Italian lorry drivers and tourists driving through the mountain roads. It was a pretty little café – the whole front entrance was completely covered with an overgrowth of wisteria; it looked lovely.

Leaping off the rocket board, I remember seeing lots of pretty birds hanging out by the café's front door, just waiting to be fed. Sasha gave them ripped up broken bits of bread every morning.

One of the little birds had a red chest and a little bomber hat on. He looked very familiar; I was sure I'd seen him somewhere before.

Then the wizard legend graced us with his presence. Sonic Sasha walked out the front door singing Bohemian Rhapsody with his bold passionate heart. He held a little bread basket in his hand but when he saw Betty, he dropped it and shouted her name out with all his might. His 'lion-like' voice echoed through the mountains.

"BETTEEEEEEEEEEEEEEEEEEE," he roared. This was a very emotional reunion for the both of them. They cried, hugged and sobbed all over each other; it was quite sweet really.

Then I noticed something funny about Sasha's tears; they behaved in a rather topsy-turvy fashion. Instead of rolling down the face, they rolled up the face. I don't know if this happens to all wizards, but it did with Sasha. His tears rolled up to the top of his head and gradually seeped into his brain, nourishing his thoughts. Wizard tears prevent hair from turning grey, which is quite excellent when you think about it.

Betty truly had no idea that Sasha had been living out in Italy for years and years; she really believed he was dead. Sasha felt terrible about this, but it was the only way to stay one step ahead of Roaring Meg. She wanted to kill Sasha so badly for trapping all her mini witches.

When the tears stopped rolling, and Betty and

Sasha finally stopped hugging, Sasha turned to me and gave me a big high five.

"Nice to meet you, little girl," he said. He was very hospitable; Betty quickly introduced us.

"Let me give you guys a quick tour of my pad." Sasha took us in and showed us all around. The ground floor was just for coffees and snacks, and the first floor was a charming little restaurant with a nice back kitchen – mainly used by tourists in the summer months. The second floor was Sasha's private living space, a nice snazzy apartment, and above that was a cosy little roof terrace, which had a pink Jacuzzi, an old wooden picnic bench and a little greenhouse with solar panels. Sasha grew all his own herbs and spices up there.

When we got back down to the ground floor, I suddenly felt quite warm, so I took my jacket off, and that's when Sasha saw the blood on my ripped T-shirt.

"Ahhhh, so you're the one who's given my rib a new home, eh?"

His bass-like voice was awfully powerful, and his eyes were different colours – one was light blue, and the other was dark green. Sasha didn't really look like a wizard. He certainly didn't dress like one; he wore faded blue jeans and a navy T-shirt.

He suddenly dropped down to one knee and readied himself to say something to me.

"Louise, I would just like to say that I am terribly sorry to drag you into all this craziness, and I'm deeply sorry about your rib being removed. That must have been an awfully painful experience for you?" He then turned to Betty.

"My darling daughter, Betty. I would also like to offer my deepest apologies to you too. Please forgive me for being so secretive all these years. I just couldn't let anyone know I was living out here; it would have been too dangerous for you and me."

Sasha became emotional again. He coughed a couple of times to try and cover up his feelings.

"I would be very honoured if you two lovely ladies joined me for lunch." Sasha smiled graciously. It was impossible for him to hide his love for Betty. Every time he looked at her, his eyes lit up like fireworks.

"Lunch sounds lovely!" I said.

"Yes, I agree," said Betty, in her lady-like voice.

Then a question suddenly popped up in my head.

"What about Roaring Meg?" I asked. "Isn't she up on the moon right now trying to free all those nasty mini witches?"

Sasha started to laugh.

"She most certainly is, Louise, but I wouldn't worry too much about her. It's going to be extremely difficult for Meg to open that marble prison." Sasha giggled wildly like an excited child.

"I made an adjustment spell, you see."

Betty and I looked at each other with curious eyes.

"What's an adjustment spell?" I asked.

"It's easy to understand," he said. "I've called this particular spell, the 'INTERNET FRUSTRATION SPELL'. Now, let me explain. Please sit."

Sasha gestured us towards the round coffee table that sat just outside the main entrance of the cafe. We parked our bums down, and Sasha began to explain.

"Well, the only time I go online is when I need to order sugar and coffee for the cafe, but the internet is so slow up here in the mountains; it drives me nuts. I know wizards ought to be patient, but I have no time for stuff like that." Sasha suddenly darted off into the café and came back in a flash with three small glasses of iced tea, then he continued.

"I was on the internet ordering stuff about a year ago, and I had just quit smoking, so I wanted to be doing something with my hands. I decided to constantly throw an old baseball up against the wall, just to catch it again and again – just something to do – to keep myself busy, you know. I waited and waited for my 'stock-up' order to say, 'ORDER COMPLETE', but as more time went by, I guess my patience just ran out. After thirty minutes, I became so angry with my slow internet that I started squeezing the baseball as hard as I could. I unconsciously started using it as a stress ball. I squeezed that baby with all the strength I had, and to my surprise, it grew in size. My goodness, it grew to the size of a basketball."

We all stopped and sipped our ice tea at the same

time, then we laughed. Sasha continued.

"That huge ball got completely filled up with all my anger and frustration, but now it was too big, so I decided to crush it into fine dust, then I placed all the dust in a shoe bag and gave it to Max. Max then took it up to the moon and sprinkled all the INTERNET FRUSTRATION DUST over the main gates of the marble prison."

Sasha was giggling again. He fell off his stool laughing uncontrollably, like a hyena, then he quickly got back up and explained himself.

"I put two spells on that dust: the first part of the spell was to keep the prison gates closed, and the second part of the spell was to curse whoever comes along, by infecting them with all the anger and frustration in the dust." Sasha was in hysterics.

"Poor old Meg. She doesn't know what's going to hit her. It's going to take her a long time to open those huge doors, that's for sure, and she's going to get really angry and frustrated while she tries. She's going to feel riddled beyond reason, ha." Sasha was very pleased with himself, so much so that he jumped up and started dancing in the road, and after a few seconds, a young Italian kid came zooming past on a fast motorbike. He just missed Sasha, phew wee.

Betty rolled her eyes up at her zany father's behaviour, then she asked, "How long will this INTERNET FRUSTRATION SPELL last, Daddy-O?"

"About three days. Don't worry, my love. We have more than enough time."

Now it was my turn to ask a question.

"Sasha, you said MAX took all the dust to the moon. Well, I'm curious. Who is Max?"

Sasha suddenly stopped dancing, put his finger and thumb up to his lips, whistled out loud, and in less than two seconds, a little red robin flew over and landed on Sasha's shoulder.

"This is Max Redwood. He's a super confident little red-chested robin from London. I found Max about ten years ago; he was dead on the road about half a mile away from the coffee shop. Poor Max had been squashed into the tarmac by a big Italian lorry. I felt sorry for the little fellow, so I decided to use some purple magic on him. I wanted to bring him back to life."

Sasha closed his eyes tightly, he concentrated like an old man digging out a dusty memory from the back of his mind.

"Ah yes, I remember exactly what happened now. I only wanted to give Max a tiny dose of purple magic, just enough to give him the gift of life, but I accidentally released a supersonic hurricane sneeze at the exact same time I put the spell on Max, so he ended up with maybe a hundred times more purple magic than he actually needed. That's why he's turned out to be such an excellent little robin, with lots of superpowers; that sneeze was the best mistake I ever made."

Sasha rambled on.

"Max can fly faster than a speeding bullet, he can breathe underwater, speak ten different languages, carry logs, make crisps, serve customers, make cappuccinos, and he keeps the greenhouse very clean. He's also very talented in the kitchen – he makes a mean minestrone soup and a Crackerjack lasagna. Speaking of food, I think it's about time we have our lunch."

Sasha started singing a silly song.

"Oh, Lunchtime with Betty, do you fancy some spaghetti? Cos that's what you're gonna-getti. Wiggly spaghetti, for Louise and Betty, a squeeze of lemon if you're hot and sweaty, and there's parmesan cheese for

Louise, if you please. Ha ha!"

Sasha was so happy. Betty had a big sunny smile on her face too. It was an absolute pleasure hanging out with these cool cosmic cats.

I had to pinch myself – one minute I was off to the laundrette to wash my school clothes on a wet cold lonely night, and now I was about to have lunch in the Italian mountains with a cool wizard and his beautiful eccentric daughter. I was also in the presence of a living legend, Max Redwood the magnificent robin; I was having a great time.

Sasha suddenly dashed back into his coffee bar and shot upstairs to the restaurant. He moved like a jumpy monkey; lunch was on its way.

We remained seated at the coffee table outside. It was cool and breezy out, but none of us really cared because the sun was on our skin. Mmmmmmm, it was toasty.

We had vegetable soup for starters.

"Get it while it's hot," shouted Sasha. It was scrumptious. Then came the main course: magnificent meatballs served with fresh wiggly spaghetti. Everything was covered by a blizzard of parmesan cheese. All this beautiful fresh Italian food really hit the spot; it was super yummy in the tummy. Then I suddenly noticed how the spaghetti moved about on my plate.

"What's that all about? Why's the spaghetti moving?" I asked.

"Ah, don't worry about that," said Sasha. "That's just a tiny pinch of purple magic mixed with fresh lime juice. It makes the pasta wiggle about like dancing worms, it gives the dish a nice ping-ting, whizz-kick taste."

The spaghetti wiggled about in my tummy like worms dancing to disco music; it was a tickly affair.

After we ate, Sasha stood up and made a small announcement – he wanted to tell us about his strange cooking habits.

"I have two types of meatballs," he said. "First, I have the delicious kind we have all just enjoyed."

Sasha then snapped his fingers, and Max flew off to the kitchen.

"The other type I have are these new ones – they are exploding meatballs!" Max flew back out with a huge salad bowl perfectly balanced on his little robin head; the bowl was filled with extra-large exploding meatballs.

"These exploding meatballs will help us defend ourselves against the crazy mini witches, they explode into sleeping smoke. The smoke contains sleeping dust, and this will instantly knock any witch out cold. We can definitely use these meatballs on the mini witches. I also have some exploding sausages, I call them bangers, they work just like the meatballs." Sasha's voice suddenly became more serious.

"A battle is coming my dear compadres, and the witches are going to be knocking on our door very soon, I have no doubt about this, they want to take over the world, they're going to want to fight and kill us, but have no fear, because I have a wham-bam-killer-plan. We are going to call on The Fuzz Cats and The Paradox Twins!"

I had no idea what Sasha was talking about.

"What's a Fuzz Cat?" I asked.

Standing behind me Sasha gently placed his hands on my shoulders and gave me a three-second shoulder rub.

"I will tell you all about these magnificent weirdos soon, my dear, but right now, it's time for some dessert, followed by coffee and biscuits."

Max suddenly flew off into the café again and came back with a silver dessert tray balanced on his head, homemade tiramisu – yummy – but he accidentally dropped it on Betty's head, oops-a-daisy!

Betty looked like she'd just lost a passionate food fight. We helped clean her up in no time; she saw the funny side of it, thank goodness. Hardly any of the tiramisu went to waste. I'm pleased to report that Max was more successful delivering the coffees and biscuits.

Over coffee, Sasha explained how he had a fantastic plan – he called it his master plan. I will tell you more about that soon. Sasha continued rambling on.

"First, I need Betty and Max to go fetch The Fuzz Cats and The Paradox Twins. This will probably take twenty-four hours because they're not just around the corner. The Fuzz Cats live in East London and The Paradox Twins live in two separate locations: one lives in Alaska, and the other lives at the bottom of the Atlantic Ocean." Sasha had great confidence in his plan.

"Louise, I would like you to stay here with me, please. The last couple of days of your life have been quite wild and weird, to say the least; you've definitely earned yourself a nice little break. You can help me in the kitchen, if you like. I'm going to prepare a big feast for when everyone returns."

Sasha got up, cleared the table and started walking back into the coffee shop, when he suddenly stopped and turned around to share some great words of wisdom,

"The time has come for us to create a tenacious gang," he spritefully agreed with himself.

"YES, A BOOMBASTIC-HARDCORE TENACIOUS GANG." He raised his fist up high and punched the air.

"TEAMWORK MAKES THE DREAM WORK, BABY. C'MON MY SON!' he said.

Then he disappeared off into the coffee shop, only to come back out with a piece of paper in his hand.

"Here you go, Betty. This is the full address of The Fuzz Cats in East London."

Betty knocked her coffee back, hopped up on her jet-powered rocket board, typed the address into her mini sat nav-system, and flew off like a golf ball being whacked down the fairway. Max Redwood took flight as well, zooming off right behind her. Betty headed straight for London, and Max headed for Alaska.

CHAPTER 10
CHARGE THOSE BATTERIES UP

Sasha and I walked back into the coffee bar and headed straight upstairs towards the kitchen. He suggested I go up to the roof terrace and just chill; he knew I needed some rest, plus he wanted to get to work on preparing his big feast.

I enjoyed a lazy afternoon on that luxurious balcony. It was a lovely feeling just resting under the sun; it charged my batteries right up.

The strong scent of the mint leaves pulled my nose over to the greenhouse. I walked in and had a good look around. My goodness, it was awfully muggy inside; a bit too moist for me, so I came back out.

Then I saw the main attraction in the other corner – the pink Jacuzzi.

"Oh yes! I've got to have a go in that," I said to myself. I shouted downstairs to Sasha and asked if I could have a dip.

"Of course," he said. "Knock yourself out."

After half a minute, Sasha threw a big sports bag up to me.

"Here you go," he shouted. The sports bag was

filled with soft towels and a big navy dressing gown – perfect.

Sasha stayed in the kitchen for ages, cooking up a storm of treats. I couldn't see him, but I heard his happy singing all through the afternoon; it lingered up the stairs, it was a delightful background noise; his cheery vocal vibes kept me company for a couple of hours. Sasha reminded me so much of Betty.

Sweet heavens above, the hot Jacuzzi was so nice; in fact, it was a bit too relaxing.

When I couldn't take any more, I stepped out and slipped into the navy dressing gown, then I walked down into Sasha's apartment. I sat back on a nice comfortable Italian sofa and closed my eyes; it took me about six seconds to slip into a deep sleep. My goodness, I slept for sixteen solid hours. I had no idea how tired I was. I woke up in the exact same position, sprawled out on the comfy sofa.

I found myself under a big soft duvet; Sasha must have chucked it over me last night. I was still in a sleepy, dopey, dreamy state of mind, but after taking a few deep breaths, I stood up, had a good long stretch, and went downstairs to wish Sasha a good morning.

Walking through the restaurant area, I noticed a lovely burning fireplace in the corner. It whispered lots of cosy crackling popping sounds; it made the whole room feel warm and homely.

I soon found Sasha in the kitchen making breakfast.

"Good morning, Louise. Did you sleep well?" Sasha had the radio on; he was listening to old rock songs.

"I reckon the rest of the gang will be back with us today, definitely before sundown."

"Good morning," I said. "Sounds good to me, I look forward to meeting all of them, I slept like a baby thanks, Sasha." I was still very sleepy. I needed about ten more minutes to wake up properly.

"Would you like some octopus tentacles on toast?"

"Wow, I've never had a breakfast like that before. I think I'll give it a try." This type of breakfast had a real twing-twang-twist to it, get ready taste buds.

"Would you like some wasabi, just to spice it up a little?"

"Oh no, thanks," but then I paused.

"Oh, go on then, maybe just a little bit."

"Yes, that's the spirit," said Sasha.

"It's good to come out of your comfort zone from time to time." I agreed with Sasha, but this time the wasabi was too much. I had to quickly gulp down a cold glass of water; straight after that Sasha made me a bowl of corn flakes, I waited till the flakes were just right, not too crispy and not too soggy, they had to be in the milk just the right amount of time, Italian milk tasted different from English milk.

Sasha's kitchen was full of character. I looked around and noticed a picture of Max Redwood on the fridge.

"Hey Sasha, would you mind telling me more about Max Redwood, please?"

"Yes, of course, I'd be happy to," he said.

"Max originally comes from Suffolk in England, but he's the type of character who gets bored easily, hence he flew out to Italy looking for some new adventures."

Sasha then poured me a nice cold glass of tropical fruit juice.

"Max fell in love with Italy as soon as he arrived; he loves the warm weather and the fresh bread. He sleeps in the greenhouse most nights."

"Here, Louise, help me with this pasta sauce please. I need you to stir it for me – just keep stirring for the next ten minutes."

I was happy to help Sasha. It was fun being in the kitchen with a wizard; he had many dishes on the go. He chopped up some onions and garlic while he rambled on about Max.

"Max is happy in Italy – he loves it here. He likes to sunbathe in the afternoons, and this has turned his orange chest to a more scarlet colour."

Sasha now turned his attention to making a huge supersize thin-crust pizza.

"Max once told me how he still loves going back to England, just once a year to visit his folks. He loves getting a good lungful of the old English countryside air.

He's got a very interesting home back in Suffolk; his folks still live there today. It's an old rusty broken-down tractor, it sits undisturbed in the corner of a huge field, looking tatty and abandoned on the outside; but on the inside, it's a secret custom-made luxurious apartment kitted out for robins. Piece by piece Max removed the engine and made his own furniture; he ripped all the sponge out from the tractors driver seat and turned it into tiny 'robin-size' beds and armchairs. The tractor house is safe, comfortable and well-hidden." Sasha pointed to another photo on the fridge door.

"Look." It was a picture of Max standing proudly on top of his tractor-house. Sasha continued.

"An old run down tractor is a pretty good place for a family of robins to live. Max has always been a resourceful little fellow. He once found an old electric blanket dumped in a skip, in someone's front garden. He took it home, trimmed it down, and connected it to the car battery that was still wired up to the tractor. Like magic, the electric blanket heated the apartment up instantly; it was perfect for cold winter nights. That blanket kept their secret home warm for many days and nights. He's a brainy one, old Max."

Sasha also told me that Max has many cousins back in England, and sometimes they all come to Italy to visit Max for their summer holidays, so Max built them a hotel – how cool is that? It sits on an old railway sleeper just next door to the cafe.

It was crystal clear to see that Sasha loves his little robin buddy. They were very good company for each other.

CHAPTER 11
THE PARADOX TWINS

I spent the last half hour stirring the pasta sauce while Sasha happily rambled on.

"I think it's time for some ice cream,' Sasha boldly announced.

He reached into the freezer and pulled out some homemade high-quality mint-choc chip Italian ice cream. He quickly filled up two bowls and topped them off with crushed cashew nuts mixed with chocolate sauce. Holy smoke, it was molto buona – magnifico! I had most definitely come to the right place.

I perched myself up on a kitchen stool and got busy scoffing, then I asked Sasha to tell me all about The Paradox Twins.

"Sure, I'd be happy to tell you about the Paradox Twins," he said, with ice cream all over his lips. "We need to go way back in time to fully understand how these two dudes actually came about."

Sasha coughed to clear his throat.

"Ok, Louise, listen carefully. It was early March in 1964 when Roaring Meg carried out some rather radical experiments, all in her North London witch cave. Her plan was to make a 'key' that would successfully open the marble prison door. She created a new key almost every night, and flew up to the moon prison with her fingers crossed. She tried and tried to open the huge door, but nothing ever happened. She never succeeded because all her keys were completely rubbish!" Sasha laughed out loud.

"Feeling completely defeated, Meg would fly back to her witch cave and go completely berserk with pure witch rage – she'd smash and obliterate everything. This became a regular routine for Meg; it seemed like she was losing her marbles. She'd get so angry that her eyes turned to a deep fiery red colour, then one day they just stayed that way."

Sasha knew he had my complete attention because I had ice cream spilled all down my navy dressing gown, and I didn't even notice. He just smiled at me and went on with the story, explaining things nice and slowly.

"Meg sadly ended up becoming a heavy whiskey drinker, but this only made matters worse – it was like she turned into the Queen of Rage. It got to the point where she was so sick of making rubbish keys that she decided to try something completely different, and this was the day she attempted to make two supersonic bodyguards, but they ended up becoming The Paradox Twins. I will explain how it all happened.

"Using two large test tubes, Meg got busy with a

wide range of unorthodox ingredients: things like crocodile blood, crushed tiger teeth, wolf claws soaked in wolf blood mixed with apple cider vinegar, seaweed from the Bermuda Triangle, vampire bones, a dead lion's tongue, hard bogies from a dead grizzly bear's nose, piranha fish teeth, some hair from Albert Einstein's moustache, wasp blood, stingray skin, and some chopped up electric eels!"

Sasha was still enjoying his ice cream. I was taking a break from mine; I had a mouth-freeze.

"Now, on the morning of the big 'BODYGUARD EXPERIMENT', Meg stupidly drank three bottles of whiskey, and after lunch, she downed a bottle of vodka. Her drinking had gotten way out of control." Sasha suddenly looked straight into my eyes and said, "It's never a good idea to perform a dangerous science experiment when you're completely drunk on whiskey, especially when you're using magic and witch spells." Sasha tapped his ice cream spoon firmly against mine. Clink!

"Science, magic and whiskey don't mix well, that's a fact, Jack." Sasha gave me a swift stern wink, then he continued.

"Meg's approach to this experiment was completely unprofessional – a perfect example of tragic magic. Instead of creating two supersonic bodyguards, she accidentally created two highly unorthodox creatures, and these guys turned out to be, The Paradox

Twins.

"Now, lots of people say that The Paradox Twins are just two scary characters from old scary bedtime and campfire stories, but the truth is, they are real – they really do exist, Louise."

"The first Paradox Twin goes by the name of Leon. He's a fierce blood-thirsty wolfman – a very wild virile creature indeed – half werewolf, half vampire, a hairy beast with extremely large fangs, and he's probably got some lion blood running in his veins. He can walk through fire and go a whole year without food. His eyes are icy blue, his face looks like old tree bark, and he's ridiculously strong.

"Over the years, many men have tried to hunt him down and kill him, but no one ever succeeded. He's been shot many times, but he will never die because he's unkillable.

"His heart is made of pure liquid silver. Now there's an old saying that says the only way a werewolf can be killed is with a silver bullet, but that rule doesn't apply to Leon. Every time Leon takes a silver bullet to the chest, it just melts into liquid and travels straight to his heart, silver bullets only make him stronger. The vampire side of Leon is very strong too. He's quite fond of blood; sometimes, he eats Alaskan bears.

"Leon escaped from Meg's witch cave when he was just one month old. He decided to live in Alaska because it's nice and peaceful out there, and he's been living there for the last fifty years, in an old deserted church, in the middle of an old sequoia tree forest. Nobody seems to bother him these days because no one ever goes there, he lives off the grid, but Max knows exactly where he is; Max will find him and bring him back."

"Wow! That's cool," I said.

"Look! There he is! That's Leon, outside!" Sasha pointed out the window.

"Where?" I asked. My heartbeat sped up as I tried to catch a glimpse of this wolf man. I looked out the window, but saw no one, and by the time I sat back on my stool, I saw that Sasha had successfully stolen the remainder of my mint-choc chip ice cream.

"Ha ha! Just kidding."

"Good one, Sasha, you got me there."

I suddenly started thinking hard about Leon.

"Poor Leon," I said. "It must get awfully lonely in that Alaskan forest."

I felt nervous about this vampire wolf man; it sounded like he was a first-class beast. The Beast from the East: that's what they call him in America. The strange thing was, Leon was coming to join us for dinner.

"I hope he has nice table manners," I said to Sasha, the old wizard picked up my nervous feelings about meeting Leon.

"Ahhhh, don't worry about Leon," Sasha remained cool and calm.

"I know how to handle him. He just needs a bit of love, that's all; he needs a father figure. I'll keep a good eye on him. Some freshly cooked Italian food will straighten him out."

I had a new job in the kitchen now – Sasha put me in charge of all the salad. He gave me a small kitchen knife and ordered me to chop up all the baby tomatoes, cucumbers and iceberg lettuce.

"Be careful with that knife, Louise – it's a sharp

little cutter!" I took caution and started chopping.

After a few minutes of kitchen doodling and listening to old gold rock songs on the radio, Sasha got busy making a fresh lasagna, then he went on to tell me about the other Paradox Twin.

"Ok, Louise, now I will tell you all about Tigerlips, Leon's brother. He's a strange ferocious sea cat who is approximately one-third tiger, one-third electric eel, and one-third stingray.

"Drunk or sober, Roaring Meg had arrived at the foregone conclusion that she hashed up the 'bodyguard experiment' big time. It was a complete and total disaster. She decided to get rid of Tigerlips by dropping him into the River Thames. He was only three weeks old, and no bigger than a kitten, but he survived because his spirit was strong. The powerful currents of the Thames dragged Tigerlips straight out to the estuary of the open sea, but he just kept on swimming and swimming, and he soon developed his own hunting skills, catching fish every day. Tigerlips grew to love the ocean; it's his home, he's been living out at sea his whole life.

"He now lives in the deepest coldest parts of the Atlantic Ocean, right at the bottom, on the seabed. He created his home in the tatty remains of the old Titanic shipwreck."

Sasha's head suddenly bowed down, like he was at a funeral. He felt sad for Tigerlips because this seacat was always alone.

"Staying inside that old shipwreck is no place to live, Louise. It's dark, cold and spooky down there. Who wants to be living all alone down at the bottom of the freezing cold ocean? It's not natural – that shipwreck is a ghostly old tomb."

Sasha suddenly moved in closer. He wanted to whisper some 'top secret' information into my ear.

"Louise, I want to tell you something. I've been secretly stashing lots of purple magic down in that shipwreck, for many years now. This is my way of helping Tigerlips – the purple magic helps him stay sharp and strong."

I understood exactly what Sasha meant because I now had purple magic in my system, his rib saved my life, and it felt great. It was like having electricity in my bloodstream."

Sasha explained things in more detail.

The Titanic (The home of Tigerlips)

"Max Redwood has secretly been delivering small doses of purple magic to that old ship for years now. I knew that, one day, I was going to need that weird cat for something. Tigerlips is going to be a unique member of our tenacious gang. All the purple magic down there has soaked into the ship's steel, and it's also gotten under Tigerlip's skin; this is the main reason why he still likes living down there today. The old shipwreck now has a positive force-field around it – it's got invisible purple magic all over it, yeah baby."

Sasha was pleased with himself, he suddenly stood up straight and smiled, looking like a superhero having his picture taken for Hello magazine. He gently tapped on his nose and gave me a quick wink. I understood what he was saying – mom's the word, be hush hush about the secret, don't tell a soul.

Sasha started whistling as he chopped up some red peppers. He was a very happy wizard, but he couldn't keep still to save his life; that was probably the coffee – he drank lots of coffee, just like Betty. Sasha suddenly stopped chopping and reached over to adjust the oven. This was a spooky moment for me because the knife he let go of continued chopping the peppers all by itself. Wizard magic is coooool.

I felt I needed to say something to Sasha.

"The Paradox Twins sound like a couple of dark dudes, but they're awfully interesting."

"Yes, they are VERY dark dudes indeed. The trouble is, they both feel completely abandoned and ripped off by Meg, and they're still extremely angry with her. Given the chance, they would probably take her head off!"

Sasha was smiling but he was on the money – he

told the exact truth.

"Ah, they'll be all right," he said.

"They just need a pack to belong to – we can help with that."

Sasha went on to explain how The Paradox Twins get stronger when they hang out together. They're already physically strong individuals, but when they're together a powerful connection comes into play, they're like a lethal force of nature, and they also have very high IQs.

I was very pleased to know that these dangerous guys were going to be on our side and not with the witches.

Sasha sipped on his expresso and spoke up some more.

"As I said earlier, Tigerlips and Leon were created in early March back in 1964. I know they always get together to celebrate their birthdays, so with a bit of luck, they'll both be in Alaska; this will make things easier for Max. He'll find the both of them at Leon's old church in the sequoia forest – they'll be playing cards and smoking big cigars.

"I know The Paradox Twins will be happy to join forces with us, Louise. I don't think they want to be outsiders anymore."

Sasha suddenly squeezed my shoulder.

"They'll be happy to be part of our new tenacious gang." He smiled, then he started looking out the kitchen window for a long time. He gazed and gazed for a good five minutes, like a poet absorbing inspiration, then he delivered a little speech.

"A wild tenacious gang, crazy and strong enough to stand up to Roaring Meg, and all her twisted mini witches." He took a deep breath and sighed gracefully.

"Yes, that's us." It almost sounded like a prayer. I patted Sasha on the back.

"You da man, Sonic Sasha!" I said, trying to be extra confident. Sasha smiled down at me, then he suddenly looked up to the ceiling. He was digging out some more old memories; and the light in his eyes suddenly became brighter.

Leon's flying motorbike

"Ah yes, I remember now. Three years ago, I gave a nice Christmas present to Leon – a flying Triumph motorbike called 'IRON JOHN'. It's a gutsy runner with an aerodynamic sidecar. Betty built this unique vehicle for me back in 1969, but I never really used it all that much, so I gave it to Leon. IRON JOHN will get them here safely."

Sasha stopped talking for a while and directed his attention to all the yummy dishes he was preparing. Authentic rich aromas of fresh Italian food filled the air, then I suddenly got hit by a feeling inside. It was like a kind of awakening – a new awareness of a new connection. I suddenly realized that I felt everything Sasha felt. This was a gift from my new rib; the rib WAS a part of Sasha, after all.

I felt that Sasha genuinely wanted to help Leon and Tigerlips; he's a damn cool wizard with a big bold heart. He knew too well that these twins were a couple of weirdos destined to become heroes. It was just a matter of time.

CHAPTER 12
THE FUZZ CATS

I wonder how Betty's getting on?" I asked.

"I'm sure she's all right. She's probably on her way back with The Fuzz Cats by now."

"What is a Fuzz Cat, Sasha?" I was terribly curious.

"Follow me up to the greenhouse, and I'll tell you all about them. I need to pick some more herbs for the pasta sauce."

"Sure, ok," I said.

So, up to the roof terrace we went. We spent only two minutes in the greenhouse, then we sat on the old wooden picnic bench.

"Let's stay up here for a while, Louise. It's really nice out today." I agreed. It was a crisp blue sky day.

"Ok, now I will tell you all about The Fuzz Cats. The Fuzz Cats are four brothers who grew up in East London – their names are Brian, Bruce, Sam and George. Their dad's name is JJ and their mum's name is Rose. Rose makes the best cup of tea in London, by the way."

Sasha reached forward to open the big red and white stripy umbrella that sat in the middle of the picnic bench; we needed shade from the Italian sunshine.

"Now, these four brothers all worked hard for their dad in the family business – a household removal company. Every morning, they all jumped in the same removal truck and drove off to work, moving different families from one house to another."

Sasha suddenly jumped up.

"Oh, pants! Sorry, Louise, I almost forgot. I need to pop down to the kitchen and put these herbs in the pasta sauce – I'll be back in a jiffy." He quickly dashed off downstairs, and made it back in under sixty seconds. He was fast and silent, like a ninja who worked in a library.

"Ok, so now I will tell you how these four nice brothers got transformed into The Fuzz Cats. It all happened in September, back in 1966. There's a black cat involved in this story too – his name is Mungo. I think I will tell you about him first.

"Mungo belonged to Roaring Meg, the crazy psycho witch. He was quite a boring old cat, completely stupid and very lazy, but no matter where Meg went, he always followed. Unfortunately, Meg's drinking made a turn for the worse in 1966. She had too much time on her hands; she was basically bored out of her knickers, ha ha." Sasha giggled loudly under the shade of the umbrella.

"Back in '66, Meg never owned a black flying surfboard – she was more traditional back then – she flew about on an old broomstick with Mungo sitting behind her.

"Meg's black flying surfboard came along years later. It was invented by a groovy Californian professor who surfs every weekend, but that's another story.

"Meg's relationship with the booze had become so dark and ugly that she drank four bottles of whiskey every day; she had turned into a creature of many bad habits. Her most dangerous habit was drinking and flying at the same time. She wasn't tipsy – she was completely smashed, these wild drunk flights always made Mungo nervous."

Sasha looked at me as he rolled his eyes up.

"Another unpleasant habit of hers was eating pigeons."

Sasha sarcastically stuck his tongue out, tilted his head back and pointed two of his fingers down into his mouth, then he continued.

"One Sunday afternoon, the four brothers were hanging out down Hackney Marshes playing football. They had no idea that Meg was flying high above them, chasing a pigeon for lunch. Mungo was up there too, hanging onto Meg's broomstick.

"The panicking pigeon flapped all over the place; he tried his best to keep away from Meg's hungry mouth. He flapped wildly, then he suddenly performed a spectacular nosedive into a grove of trees. This all took place just a stone's throw away from where the four brothers were playing. The pigeon suddenly slipped a quick, slick double-kick backflip, but Meg was already waiting right behind him. She made her move and snatched the pigeon right out of the air, then she scoffed him up in two seconds flat."

"Mamma mia, that's disgusting," I said.

"Exactly!" said Sasha. "Let me tell you what happened to the cat. When the pigeon was halfway through his double-kick-backflip, Meg moved faster than lightning to catch the dopey pigeon off-guard, but poor Mungo wasn't ready for this fast move – he slipped, lost his grip and crash-landed head first into a massive oak tree. The collision made a huge THUD sound; Mungo was knocked out cold, lying on the ground; looking like he was sunbathing on the grass.

"Meg knew nothing about this. She thought her little black cat was still on the back of the broomstick, but he was long gone.

"The four brothers heard the thud and saw Mungo lying on the grass, they all rushed over to investigate. Mungo was still breathing, so they quickly took him home and put him in the care of their mum, Rose. She nursed him back to good health in no time.

"Now, not many people know this, Louise, but some witches use their cats for magic storage."

I looked at Sasha with a curious face. He went on.

"It's simple – the witch keeps all their magic stored up inside their cat's body. The cat is completely unaware of this, of course. This was the case with Mungo. There was a huge amount of witch magic stored inside him, but only Meg knew about this."

Sasha suddenly stopped his storytelling to take his shoes and socks off. My goodness, his feet were so stinky! I quickly suggested that he dip them in the Jacuzzi tub; Sasha did just that, he then continued with the story.

"As time went by, Mungo became accepted as the new family pet. All the four brothers had grown very fond of him. Mungo ended up going to work every morning with the boys – he was part of the gang now. Always the first one to hop up into the big removal lorry, he loved looking out the front windscreen, wondering what adventures the day might bring. His long black tail happily whipped about as he purred in harmony with the heavy hum of the lorries engine.

"Then, one day, JJ and his four sons took on a huge removal job that would change all their lives forever.

"JJ and all the brothers moved a rich old man out of a big house in Hampstead, North London. They took all his stuff to his new home on the Isle of Wight, where he bought a lovely windmill close to the beach.

"Now, the coolest thing about the house in Hampstead was the beautiful swimming pool in the back garden.

"The four brothers overheard that the Hampstead house was going to be empty for three days, so they planned a midnight break-in just to have a free swim in the backyard."

"Oh, I say, they are cheeky!"

"Yes, four cheeky little raccoons, ha ha," Sasha laughed wildly for just one second, then he rambled on some more.

"The move to the Isle of Wight was a piece of cake. As soon as they got back to London, they drove up to the big empty house, climbed over the side gate, and headed straight for the pool. It was a naughty thing to do, but these brothers didn't care – they just wanted to have some fun. It wasn't like they were stealing anything.

"Mungo wanted to have some fun too; the behaviour of that crazy cat was very surprising. Cats don't usually swim, but Mungo was the exception. Just like the four brothers did, Mungo jumped in and out of that pool all night long; they were all having a blast.

"Then, halfway through the night, the brothers ordered themselves an extra large deep-pan Hawaiian pizza, which they scoffed up in no time. Soon after that, the night got colder. It was already cold outside, but now it was freezing cold, and a thunderstorm came their way. The boys didn't really care – they carried on doing their bombs and somersaults into the pool.

"A hard rain came crashing down while thunder and lightning filled the skies above. It was a fierce storm, but these boys were fearless. They pretended the thunder and lightning were disco lights sent from the heavens above; their adrenaline ran high.

"Swimming in an open-air pool under a thunderstorm may have been a fun and dangerous rock 'n' roll thing to do, Louise, but it turned out to be a crazy life-changing experience for these wild cats." Sasha winked.

"Without any warning, a huge jagged bolt of lightning stabbed its way down through the sky and hit the swimming pool with a huge whacking bazooka, zap! All the boys (and the cat) were in the water at this crucial moment.

"This turned out to be a fleeting moment of nature at its wildest – they all got completely electrocuted! Mungo the cat died instantly – he got frizzle-fried down to his bones – and slowly dissolved into the electric water. Things weren't looking much better for the four brothers. An unlimited amount of electricity poured its way down through that jagged bolt of lightning, before it snatched itself back up into the sky, then it, very unexpectedly, came zipping back down for a second zap!

"Things really started cooking now; strange chemicals and spirits swished about in the water. The witch magic stored up inside Mungo's body swirled about in that pool, along with Mungo's DNA. The four brothers were experiencing some radically intense electric-shock treatment, at an extremely sky-high voltage, but they were somehow managing to stay alive.

"The electricity in the water crept deep into their bones. They got wham-jolted and jam-slapped all over the place; they looked like they were doing some kind of crazy sizzle-sneeze dance, like this."

Sasha suddenly jumped out of the Jacuzzi tub and danced about in front of me like a silly zombie made of jelly; he looked so funny. He jolted around like he had a hyperactive squirrel trapped inside his underpants. My tummy hurt from laughing so much, then he finally sat back down at the picnic bench and continued with the story.

"It was like the swimming pool had turned into a huge cauldron of cosmic energy. There was a lot going on, Louise. Let's see now, we had electricity mixed with cold water – that got mixed with witch magic, and all that got mixed with Mungo's DNA. This powerful mixture continued swirling and swishing about, making choppy waves and strong undercurrents, zapping the four brothers into a frenzy. They got ping-trotted into a deep trance, completely zing-fired from head to toe."

"However did they survive?" I asked.

"I have absolutely no idea. That, my love, is a total mystery. They should have died in that pool, but some freaky supernatural miracle must have saved them. They underwent a huge transformation; for ten strange minutes they got slam-jammed all over that pool. It must have felt like being trapped inside a blender, but when they finally came out, they had all been successfully transformed into The Fuzz Cats. They shined vividly like the stars above; these electric guys were fully charged up now!"

Sasha's eyes lit up.

"Their hairstyles went through some funny changes too. They all looked fuzzy and bushy, their fingernails turned into cat's claws, and their ears became pointy, they all seemed to be more catty and agile; sharper in their senses – you know, like wild cougars. Mungo's DNA had found its way into their bloodstream. These Cat-boys had also absorbed all the witch magic from Mungo's belly, making them terribly powerful, but they needed time to learn how to use and master these unique powers. It was a matter of using patience and practice to develop their magically-driven skills. I am pleased to say that they've now mastered them very well; they use their powers very wisely, Louise.

I sat back and took a deep breath.

"Well, blow me down, Sasha. That transformation sounds like a pretty wild trip, I must say."

"Yes, very wild indeed," he replied.

"I'm just going down to the kitchen to check up on all the food." Sasha quickly ran off, but he was back after three minutes with two big glasses of coconut juice, then he rambled on some more.

"From that day on, the four brothers were never the same. There's no turning back for these guys now – they're going to be The Fuzz Cats for the rest of their lives, which is cool because they're secret heroes now, they could easily be described as mobile human power stations. They never get tired, and they live in a very high vibration of pure electricity, their energy readings go right off the charts.

"These guys live in a big warehouse in East London. It's in a very remote area; nobody ever disturbs them, and that's the way they like it. They only come out at night, in a big old ice cream van. They fight crime and help homeless people. In the winter months, they hand out soup to the homeless, and in the summer months, they hand out cherry-flavoured smoothies.

"Over the years, they've become highly skilled in sword fighting and karate; they are secret guardian ninja-angels of the night.

"They've helped lots of people, many times. If, for example, a man coming home late from work got jumped by a gang of angry boys, The Fuzz Cats would intervene and protect the man. They'd make sure he got home safely with his wallet and money, but they'd also help the gang of boys; they'd give 'em some money and books to read. The book they love to give away most is; 'The Power of Your Subconscious Mind' by Dr Joseph Murphy. The Fuzz Cats want to help everyone."

"That's very interesting," I said, then we both sat back and sipped on our coconut juice.

"So, now you know a little bit about The Fuzz Cats and The Paradox Twins," Sasha smiled.

I didn't know what to say, so I just raised my glass and said 'Cheers Sasha, I'm looking forward to meeting every single member of our new tenacious gang.' I was very happy to be in the presence of such a fine wizard.

"Oh, I forget to tell you – sometimes The Fuzz Cats leave their ice cream van at the warehouse, and go out on their skateboards, they usually do this in the summer months."

CHAPTER 13
KELLY ANN

Sasha never seemed to stop talking. I reckon he must have spent many years alone. It was quite pleasurable listening to him go on though; the content of his constant rambling was quite interesting. I knew it was just a matter of time before he would have something else to say.

"Louise, I have something else to say."

See, I told you.

Sasha decided to drop a news bomb and tell me about his other daughter, the wonderful Kelly Ann, a groovy chick who lives on a boat.

We had a nice light lunch on the roof terrace that afternoon: Parma ham with fresh melon.

After lunch, I suddenly saw an expression on Sasha's face that I hadn't seen before. He looked quite emotional, but this time, it was more of a sad feeling. This was going to be interesting, I thought to myself, then he spoke up.

"Louise, I would like to tell you all about my other daughter, Kelly Ann. She's an eccentric and sensitive girl who lives in Camden Town, on a Dutch barge. She has light purple hair, wears dark purple lipstick, and has a lovely little beauty spot on the tip of her nose. Her Dutch barge sits peacefully on the still waters of the Camden canal, North London. She works two minutes from home, in Camden Market, selling saxophones and roller-skates, except on Sundays when she works in an art gallery." Sasha seemed to have more energy when he spoke about his daughter. He went on.

"Kelly Ann keeps busy most evenings. Some nights she stays home and makes jewellery on her barge, and other nights she helps organise illegal races for old wrinkly people, who love driving their electric-powered motor scooters really fast. They love racing in the car park of the local cinema; it makes them feel young again. Kelly Ann also teaches lots of old people how to knit, but it's not just a plain old boring knitting circle where old people sip tea, eat biscuits, fart, dribble and moan about things; oh no. Kelly Ann combines her knitting lessons with martial arts. Kung-Fu knitting is a very useful skill for old people to have – if any young bad boys try to mug them, they get their butt kicked." Sasha sniggered.

"Kelly Ann loves baking strawberry cakes, and she's also a bit of a fortune teller; this is easy for her because she's telepathic. Her star sign is Pisces and sometimes, she talks to ghosts, but only the friendly ones. She loves blowing on her saxophone while she roller-skates through Camden High Street, but what she loves most is making old people happy."

A few tears fell from Sasha's eyes and swiftly rolled up into his hair.

"She sounds lovely, Sasha," I said. "I look forward to meeting her." She sounded like a bowl of cherries when compared to The Fuzz Cats and The Paradox Twins.

Sasha snivelled a little.

"Yes, she is lovely. In fact, she's absolutely beautiful and gorgeous." Sasha was very proud of his daughter, but he was angry with himself.

"She'll definitely be here later. Kelly Ann just knows stuff; I believe it's a gift you know. She knows we're all meeting here tonight.

"She doesn't have a mobile phone, she never watches TV, and she hardly ever spends time on social media. She prefers doing things the old-fashioned way. She enjoys chatting with her friends in the market, she absolutely loves handing out free home-made jewellery and free strawberry cakes to her customers – most of Kelly Ann's customers end up becoming friends."

"She's always got a good book on the go. She's read all the Harry Potter books six times over, but she finds it difficult to fit in. She can't believe the way so many people have their faces stuck to their phones all day long, and deep down, I think she finds it hard to accept that she's the daughter of a wizard. She gets frustrated because she has powers, but no one has taught her how to use them properly."

I listened intensely. It was plain to see that Sasha was truly upset with himself. He wanted to be closer to both his daughters, he wanted to be a better father, but the difficult circumstances of being a maverick wizard wanted by a crazy psycho witch kept them apart. He went on. "Kelly Ann's telepathy is so strong. I guarantee she'll be here tonight; she knows her presence is requested."

Sasha suddenly broke down in tears. He cried in front of me like a little boy; it was very endearing. He did that silly soppy thing when people cry and talk at the same time. I was trying my best not to laugh; I just about understood him.

"She's so pretty," he said.

"Every morning, just before she sets off to work, she puts a fresh red rose in her hair. She has such a busy and extraordinary life. I love her so much, Louise. I hope she isn't lonely – maybe she has a new boyfriend now? I hope she does." I just listened to Sasha – that's all I could do – listen without judgement as he babbled on.

"I guess you could say she's a kind of genius because she knows a little bit about everything. She's a very fast reader. She used to be dyslexic, but she just kept on reading and reading and reading, and more brain cells grew in her head, making her dyslexia get weaker and weaker.

"She knows her father is creating a tenacious gang; premonitions come to her all the time.

"She always knew I was alive out in Italy, and she

knew that she wasn't allowed to visit me, she couldn't say anything to anyone, not even Betty.

"These were very difficult circumstances for Kelly Ann to accept. She found it so hard to be happy, knowing I was alive, and having to keep away for so long; that's not fair, Louise. It's been a heavy burden for her to carry."

Poor Sasha, he so wanted to be a better more available father. I wrapped both my arms around him as he continued crying on my shoulder, every single tear ran up his forehead.

Under all this grief, he was probably quite nervous. He would soon be in the presence of both his daughters, for the first time in such a long time.

I was nervous too, about many things. I started thinking about The Paradox Twins and The Fuzz Cats; they all seemed to be so weird and freaky. I was scared in my mind but excited in my heart. Deep down inside, I was looking forward to having dinner with all these unorthodox misfits.

Sasha finally started pulling himself back together. My serviette from lunch was still sitting on the table, under a clean knife, so I gave it to Sasha to help him wipe his sniffles away, then I gave him a little kiss on the cheek and threw a big smile into his eyes; this seemed to cheer him up. He smiled back, then we both made our way back down to the kitchen. It was nice to see a fully grown man expressing his feelings.

CHAPTER 14
HERE COMES THE CAVALRY

Sasha now had a little job for me. He wanted me to rearrange all the tables and seats in the restaurant area.

"Just put them all together to make one big table in the middle of the room please, Louise." That's what he asked for, so that's what he got. I set the big table up in two minutes, it was easy, but I decided to rearrange things just one more time, pushing everything a little closer to the open log fire. I love that fire, it was the heart of the restaurant, then Sasha walked back in to inspect my work.

"Excellent!" he said. "Make sure there's lots of cutlery and plates and glasses for everyone." I had it all covered.

Then, we suddenly heard a motorbike pull up outside and some lullaby music from an old ice cream van. We then heard the roaring sound of Betty's jet-powered rocket board, and a few seconds after that, Max Redwood zoomed in through the window. He landed on my head at first, then he took off and landed on Sasha's shoulder.

"He likes you," said Sasha, as he dug into his

pocket to give Max some bird seed.

"Sounds like everyone's back," I said.

"Splendid," was all Sasha said. I think he was more focused on getting all the food ready in time. I was eager to catch a glimpse of our fantastic guests. I hurried over to the window and gazed down like a star struck fan – I was terribly excited.

Sasha walked over and stood beside me. He opened the sash window and said, "Come upstairs, everyone. Dinner will be served in ten minutes."

I couldn't believe my eyes – it looked like a Halloween gathering down there. I saw The Fuzz Cats get out of their ice cream van. My goodness, they looked like spooky rock stars, then I saw The Paradox Twins on their 'IRON JOHN' flying triumph motorbike. Leon, the cool vampire wolf man, wore a black leather jacket with black biker's goggles, but no crash helmet. His fangs looked very scary, then I saw Tigerlips, the electric stingray man, I watched him slowly climb out of the sidecar. Holy smoke, he looked weird. He looked like a tiger at first, but then he stood up and walked like a man. He had a black leather jacket on too; it was terribly worn out. These guys were amazing.

I couldn't believe I was going to have dinner with all these outcasts. It was like they all jumped out from the pages of a haunted comic book; they looked like a bunch of twisted, messed up mongrels.

Then, another vehicle suddenly pulled up – it was

the washing machine race car, The Spinner. I noticed that the driver had light purple hair. That's got to be Kelly Ann, I whispered to myself – I was right.

Like a wise, silent owl, I continued gazing down, just watching everyone with my mouth wide open. I was mesmerized with delight; this was an amazing gathering. I watched Kelly Ann and Betty greet each other with a big loving sisterly hug, then I heard Kelly Ann say something.

"Hey Sis, I hope you don't mind me taking the spinner for a spin. I needed to get out here fast." Betty gave Kelly Ann another big hug.

"Oh Honey, of course I don't mind. It's just so nice to see you. I've missed my little sis." Kelly Ann smiled brightly. She was ever so pretty.

Everyone shuffled into the coffee shop and slowly made their way upstairs. One by one, I watched them walk into the restaurant and find their seat at the big table. Sasha was truly excited to have everyone there, but I think I was more excited. My rib glowed powerfully under my T-shirt.

CHAPTER 15
A TENACIOUS GANG IS FORMED

There was a funny feeling in the air as we all sat round the big table together; it was a gritty, scratchy sort of atmosphere. All of us huddled together in one room seemed to create a crazy mixture of snappy electrical energy. I felt all the emotions of all the different guests; the main emotion I picked up was raw love mixed with a sprinkle of pain. All this energy made the log fire pop and flicker with passion, but after ten minutes, the vibes calmed down, and things became more peaceful. Our new guests were slowly letting their guards down; it's not easy for warriors to let go of their armour.

I started creating a list in my mind. The list was a detailed focus on all the different powers we had in the room: there was wizard magic, vampire-wolf powers, psychic mind powers, purple magic, witch powers, and a powerful type of electrical cat energy in the air. I think the purple magic was the strongest. I say this because my rib throbbed like I had two hearts – all this magical energy was overwhelming.

The electrical currents coming off from The Fuzz Cats seemed to buzz loudly like one of those outdoor electrical lamps, the ones that kill bugs?

Tigerlips had quite a buzzy aura around him too. Sitting next to The Fuzz Cats gave him electrostatic hair. It stretched up high like it was reaching for the stars.

Tigerlips and The Fuzz Cats became good buddies immediately. They were all on the same level because they had electricity in their catty bloodstream. I also notised how Kelly Ann couldn't take her eyes off Tigerlips. Perhaps there was some romantic electricity in the air as well, ha-ha.

Leon, the wolf man, was pretty quiet at the table. He struck me as the strong silent type; he seemed to be completely unafraid of everything. He stared at me across the table for over five minutes, and didn't blink once; he was quite intimidating, I must say. Maybe he was thinking about eating me for dessert? I stuck my tongue out at him, just to try and make him smile, but all he did was raise his eyebrows.

Betty and Kelly Ann chatted away endlessly about skin creams and hair dye. Kelly Ann said she was thinking about changing her purple hair to a light green 'aqua mermaid' colour.

Betty suggested the 'Dark green seaweed' shade, then she suddenly stroked my blue hair and told Kelly Ann how she loves the 'sky blue' effect – just girly talk I guess. Hanging out with this gang was fun.

It was time for all these individuals to come

together and work as a team. Sasha had a lot of faith in us; he believed the spirit of teamwork would bring out the best in all of us. I trusted Sasha – he was the one who knew how to get things done, and he also knew how to get tip-top results.

Sasha clapped his hands twice with authority, and everyone hushed down and sat up – dinner time had finally arrived. Using a pinch of purple magic, Sasha flew all the food out from the kitchen, making sure it landed gracefully on the big dinner table. Max brought out a tray with serviettes, salt and pepper, horseradish, mint sauce, ketchup, barbeque sauce, and gravy.

The table was now filled with yummy treats. There was Sasha's magnificent homemade lasagna and his freshly-made penne pasta, mixed with delicious homemade pesto sauce. We had wiggly spaghetti bolognese, served in a light delightful spicy herb sauce. There was smoked salmon, served on slices of French baguette bread – that was delicious.

We had bangers and meatballs (they weren't the exploding ones) served with cauliflower and broccoli, all cooked in melted stinky cheese, a massive bowl of big fat chips covered in ketchup – they were so yummy. There was another portion of fat chips on the other side of the table. They were covered in barbecue sauce – Leon ate all of them, pig.

We had Parmesan cheese and a big bowl of olive oil for everyone to dip their bread into. We had a big pizza to share, we had balsamic vinegar, lots of green and black olives, strawberry-flavoured jelly, raspberry-flavoured ice cream, bird seed (for Max), sea mussels and squid soup (for Tigerlips), and lots of coconut-flavoured smoothies. We also had a delicious blueberry and mango fruit salad, a huge jug of carrot juice (which Leon drank all to himself) and a huge salad to share (the salad dressing was a minty sauce with a twist of ginger, very tasty.

"Let's eat!" shouted Sasha. We all tucked into the magnificent feast, and after five minutes of munching and scoffing, everyone seemed to be more content and happy; the fantastic food in our bellies made all the difference. Lots of light-hearted conversation suddenly kicked off. All the gang were slowly breaking the walls down between each other – talking about the weather or how fast their vehicles could travel – then everyone started complimenting Sasha on cooking such a fine feast.

Sasha stood and bowed gracefully; he hardly spoke a word. He knew it was too early in the evening to start going on about his master plan. He just kept himself busy making sure nobody felt left out – he was a good host, an absolute gentleman. He knew everybody needed a good gut-full of food before anything else.

Then, right out of the blue, Kelly Ann stood up and made an announcement.

"Listen, guys, I need to let you all know something

143

– we have a spirit here among us."

Everyone suddenly stopped eating and there was silence in the restaurant. The fire crackled loudly as we all looked over to Kelly Ann. She continued to explain things.

"What I mean is, a ghost has joined us for dinner, but don't worry, she's all right – she's one of us. She has a strong heart, and she wants to help us. Her name is Penelope Jones, and she was once a famous boxer in North London."

My O My, I couldn't believe this. My mum used to tell me stories about this legend when I was seven years old. Penelope Jones was a crazy-ass illegal female boxer from the 1950s, and now I get to meet her – this was nuts!

Sasha told everyone to shuffle around the table, just enough to make room for one more guest – a ghost guest.

"Somebody go grab another chair for Penelope, please," he asked.

I was happy to do this. I slowly pushed the chair in towards the table, and there she was. Penelope Jones suddenly appeared, sitting comfortably right in front of me. She was as light as a feather – a featherweight, ha. Penelope was dressed in a yellow silky boxer's gown, in black fancy writing her name was embroidered on the back. She looked so old, but she was very alive; her wrinkly face reminded me of a walnut. I reached over to touch her boxing gloves, but my hands went straight through them.

"I'm a ghost, my dear. You can't touch me." Penelope suddenly stood up and started bouncing on the spot. She bopped up and down as she punched and jabbed the air in front of her. She was a cheeky old gal but very likeable.

"I like you guys," she said.

"And I wanna help y'all."

Then Sasha spoke up.

"Ok, that's lovely. Thank you, Penelope. We're very happy to have you with us. Ok, so it looks like we're all here now."

Sasha poured some red grape juice in his glass; it looked just like red wine.

"Now, before I tell you about my master plan, I want to express that I completely disagree with violence."

Everybody looked at each other with surprised facial expressions. Sasha continued.

"I know it's going to get ugly when these mini witches come down from the moon, but if we go to war with them, it will just be madness. There is nothing good about violence and war and killing; it's completely foolish. Being violent is choosing to live at the lowest level of intelligence; in fact, it's beneath intelligence."

"I agree," said Penelope. I was violent in the ring for almost all my life, and it messed me right up. I ended up with arthritis in both my knees and both my hands, and I never got to be old and happy. I died at the young age of forty-nine. If I had a more peaceful life, I'm sure I would have lived longer."

Sasha gently hushed Penelope up and ordered Max to dim the lights. Betty suddenly noticed how the fire was dying down, so she quickly fetched a new log and immediately chucked it on the fire. Sasha's strong presence and calm aura silently encouraged the whole gang to simmer down. It was time for our captain to reveal his master plan.

Now, I won't tell you every single detail about the master plan because, where's the fun in that?

I will tell you that Sasha had no intention of killing Roaring Meg or any of the mini witches. He wanted to turn the tables on everything. His plan was quite weird, but so is Sasha.

CHAPTER 16
ONE POWERFUL HEART VISIT

The first stage of Sasha's master plan included one of his favourite spells – that would be the HEART VISIT SPELL. When I first heard about this spell, I thought it was a load of rubbish, but my attitude changed when Sasha explained things in more depth.

A heart visit spell takes place when a wizard, like Sasha, turns himself into a spirit and pays a little visit to someone's heart, with the sole desire to give them strength and hope. He might stay inside someone's heart for a couple of days, but if they're going through a mega tough time, he'll stay longer. I know this to be true because Sonic Sasha stayed in my heart for two weeks, just after my folks disappeared. I knew nothing about this until recently, but looking back, it did feel like someone or something was helping me carry on.

So, the time had come for another heart visit, but this time, it was going to be a little more complicated and a lot more dangerous, excellent!

Hanging out with these fruit loops, I began to realise and accept that danger was just an everyday part of life.

This second heart visit was completely unlike Sasha's visit to my heart – this time, the whole gang was coming along. I was curious to know whose heart we were going to visit and why?

What I'm about to say now doesn't really make much sense, but it will in time.

Sasha wanted the whole gang to work as a team. He wanted us to pick up the Titanic shipwreck from the Atlantic Ocean seabed and take it over to Hudson Bay, in Canada.

The Titanic had been resting deep at the bottom of the ocean ever since it sank on the 15th April, 1912, just hours after it hit the iceberg. It would take a great deal of strength and stamina to pick this shipwreck up, but Sasha's plan was magnificent, and he believed we could do it.

Now, it was time for Sasha to tell us whose heart we were going to visit.

"Ok, guys, the heart we're all going to climb into is the mighty passionate heart of Max Redwood – The Magnificent Robin."

Everyone in the gang laughed out loud.

I mean, really? Can you imagine that? The whole gang fitting inside the little heart of a red-chested robin – it just sounds ridiculous. When the laughter finally fizzled out, everyone realised that Sasha was serious. He closed his eyes and put his hands together, and then it happened.

The strength and spirit of The Paradox Twins, The Fuzz Cats, Betty, Sasha, Kelly Ann and Penelope Jones were all about to come together in one little heart. I felt nervous for Max. Maybe this overload of majestic power was going to make his heart explode? Sasha quickly opened his eyes and said that he wanted ME to be part of this mission too. He said I was brave and pointed out how we needed all the purple magic we could get our hands on. Thanks to my new rib, there was lots of purple magic running through my bloodstream; I was happy to help out.

And, so it happened. Sasha turned all of us into smoky spirits, and soon after that, he turned our spirits into one big giant spirit. Standing confidently on his thin little robin legs, Max Redwood leaned forward and slowly breathed us in, through his little beak.

What happened next was insane.

You might be thinking that Max turned into a huge giant-size robin, but he didn't. In fact, his appearance didn't change at all, but on the inside, it was a different story altogether, for Max had now become the world's strongest creature of all time. It was like he had the strength of a million stallions. This experience was the most powerful and beautiful feeling I had ever felt.

We left Sasha's coffee bar at ten in the evening and stayed inside Max's heart for about four hours; that was enough time to get the job done.

Max swiftly flew out of Italy and headed straight

for the Atlantic Ocean. We flew at 1665 miles per hour, cutting through the sky like a feathered bullet. It took us fifteen seconds to fly over the south of France – we were well on our way.

Max flew just one metre above sea level. He loved danger. He truly was an Evel Knievel robin, then he suddenly dived into the freezing cold ocean. It was such a rush – this was a dicey mission.

We swam deeper and deeper into the darkness, until we reached the seabed. Max knew exactly where he was going. He'd gone down to visit the Titanic many times before, on his purple magic runs.

It was the strangest sensation being wrapped up in a big spirit inside Max's little heart; I would say Sasha's spirit had the strongest vibe.

Max suddenly found the shipwreck and started bashing his head into it; he needed to loosen it up first. It's important to know that the Titanic has been sitting on the seabed for many years. It wasn't easy to budge, but Max persevered. The Titanic snapped in half when it sank on that fatal night. We went for the half that Tigerlips lived in – the stern end. Max constantly rammed his little head into that ship like a wild Spanish bull, but it wouldn't budge at all.

"Come on, Max," I shouted, then everyone else joined in and yelled along with me.

"Yes, come on, Max. You can do it!" This gave Max a boost of confidence. It gave him the edge he needed; teamwork is the key.

Then it happened – the ship started moving, yes! We heard these weird, heavy, creaking noises at first. Max was slowly tilting the ship over, thousands of trapped air bubbles suddenly popped out and raced back up to the ocean's surface.

Max kept throwing himself into the side of the ship like a little mad man. He was mean, lean and ultra-keen.

"Come on, Mad Max! Give it all you've got, my son!" shouted Sasha.

Max was totally pumped!

Then I heard Betty get bossy.

"Come on, guys! This is a team effort – we're all here inside Max's little heart together, so put your backs into it! Help Max out! WE ARE ALL ONE TODAY!" she yelled.

Max continued bashing himself into the ship, when something unique happened – a mellow purple light started to reveal itself. This was all the purple magic sleeping deep inside the ships steel, it was waking up, and it soon helped make the ship become just that little bit lighter.

After a lot of tugging and heaving, Max finally rolled the ship over, and lots of sealife suddenly came dashing out. We didn't mean to flip their home upside down – sorry about that guys. We saw pink exotic fish swim off like wavy ribbons, then we saw thousands of electric blue fish swim off. They looked like tiny pieces of broken glass, then we saw lots of long, wormy, yellow fish swim off; they looked like giant caterpillars. There was another big, giant, orange fish lurking about that looked like a lost scarf. They soon disappeared off into the darkness. The purple glow of the ship gave us just enough light to see what was going on down there.

Now that the ship had successfully been flipped over, Max got himself ready to get the best grip he could find; way down at the back he almost stabbed his robin claws into the rusty old body. I felt the blood in his little heart boil up like volcano lava, then Max started lifting the whole damn shipwreck up to the top of the ocean – it was absolutely mind-blowing! I still don't understand to this day how Max did it, but some things in life, I guess, I will never understand.

Sasha BELIEVED it could be done, and that was all that mattered. I had complete faith in Sasha. It's easy to trust him because he saved my life – without his rib I'd be dead.

Now being in Max's heart with the rest of the gang is something I will never forget for the rest of my life. We all moved that ship together with pure hearty teamwork. The combined energy of all the dynamic magic on that day was absolutely phenomenal. We all heard Sasha's voice constantly shouting and yelling like a football coach who was obsessed with winning.

"Come on, guys! We've got it now! Give it everything you've got! Come on! That's it! Let's have it! Don't hold back, give it your all! Teamwork makes the dream work! Go for it! Get in there, Max!" Sasha was a great team leader. Max was happy with his grip. He flapped his little wings with pure determination.

Now, most robins usually zoom across the sky carrying twigs or worms, right? But not Max Redwood. This crazy superhero broke through the ocean's surface carrying the old Titanic shipwreck beneath him. His little robin claws were super-powerful – what a diamond geezer!

The tenacious gang had successfully injected ALL their passionate raw strength and energy into Max's little heart and body. I remember how fantastic it felt as we climbed higher and higher into the evening sky. We all felt the rush of adrenaline kick off; this was followed by a huge wave of endorphins. Max sang a sweet happy melody as he flew along the starry skies. Following orders from Sasha, we took the shipwreck directly to Hudson Bay in Canada; it wasn't too far away.

When we finally arrived, I remember seeing Hudson Bay glimmer under the dim, pale light of the moon, it wasn't a full moon, it was a crescent moon that night; it looked beautiful. Sasha knew exactly where he wanted the old shipwreck to go. He wanted it dropped back in the ocean, but not so deep this time. It had to be close to the surface, just one metre under sea level.

Max released the shipwreck from his grip about a mile out from the Canadian shore – when it hit the ocean it made the biggest splash ever. This was unbelievable, but deep down inside, I believed it. In the name of teamwork, we did it.

That was the first stage of Sasha's master plan done and dusted – mission accomplished. It was now time for us to head back to the coffee bar in Italy.

So, why would Sasha want the remains of the Titanic moved to Hudson Bay? The simple answer to that question is because it's all part of the master plan. I will explain more later but right now, all you need to know is this; Sasha wants to get rid of Roaring Meg and all the mini witches, but he doesn't want to kill them – that's not his style.

CHAPTER 17
FOLLOWING ORDERS

There was just one more thing Sasha wanted Max to do before we headed back to Italy. He instructed his feathery little friend to RIP OFF the Titanic's huge propeller and fly it over to London. The Titanic had three colossal propellers right at the back. Sasha wanted the middle one because it had an extra fin. This was a strange request, but Max did as he was told. He delivered the propeller directly to Betty's laundrette in Portobello Road, leaving it by the back door.

"Good job, Max. This propeller is going to come in very handy soon," said Sasha.

Then we all flew back to Italy.

The whole gang spending time together inside Max's little heart was an excellent way for us to create a strong bond. It felt like we'd all been crammed together inside a two-man tent. There was a team spirit among us now. I'd be happy to do another heart visit with these guys; it was a unique experience.

We arrived back at Sasha's coffee bar at two a.m. in the morning. Sasha immediately drew us out of Max's little heart with delicate skill and gentle precision. He moved fast because we had lots to do.

"Right, listen up everyone. We have a list of things to do. First off, I want Betty to do some work on The Fuzz Cat's ice cream van. Not just yet though – wait till we get back to London. There are some major adjustments to be carried out." Sasha spoke fast and hard, like an American basketball coach during a timeout.

"Everyone is coming back to Betty's London laundrette with me, except for The Paradox Twins. I have a special job for you two." Sasha explained everything as quickly as he possibly could.

"Leon and Tigerlips will be heading over to New Zealand to fetch my huge supply of purple magic. I left it there a few years ago – it's hidden in a lighthouse." Sasha wanted Leon to fly his IRON JOHN motorbike and Tigerlips to follow in the spinner. As soon as Sasha made this announcement, Betty walked Tigerlips over to the spinner and gave him some instructions on how to operate her 'one of a kind' race car. She hit the TURBO WASH button; and this automatically turned the spinner into a speedboat.

"Ok, so if you're on land and you're about to set sail, just hit the turbo wash button, and boom; you got yourself a speedboat – ok, Tiger-boy."

Tigerlips smiled and nodded to Betty,

"OK, Gotcha," was all he said, then Sasha continued.

"Getting over to New Zealand won't be a problem for a couple of rude boys like you two. The lighthouse is at Jacks Point in Timaru – this is on the South Island. There's only one lighthouse at Jack's point, so it'll be easy to find."

This New Zealand mission for The Paradox Twins seemed simple, but if any witches found out about them, the situation could get heavy and go south. All they had to do was collect an old suitcase full of magic and bring it back to London. Sounds easy enough but Sasha knew it was a risky task. Lots of mini witches will be roaming about soon, and they'll be looking for anything suspicious.

Sasha proceeded to give some instructions to Leon, while Tigerlips got familiar with all the spinner's controls and special features. Sasha had no immediate instructions for me, so I just sat back and watched everyone else. That's when I noticed a certain sweetness in the air between Kelly Ann and Tigerlips. It was official, they both had a crush on each other, ahhhh…

Betty called Tigerlips over to tell him about the fuel tank. "When you fill it up, it's best to use non-biological washing powder, ok, whatever you do, don't use biological."

"Non-biological – ok, I got it." Tigerlips listened to Betty, but he wasn't really giving his full attention to her. His gold piercing amber- eyes kept looking over to Kelly Ann, and she kept looking back at him – smiles were exchanged - love was in the air, ha ha – then Betty suddenly turned into a stroppy bossy-boots.

"Hey, pay attention, please – this is important!" She gave Tigerlips a swift gentle slap on the cheek. This made Tigerlips growl, and Kelly Ann giggle.

Sasha soon decided that he wanted someone to help The Paradox Twins on their mission, someone to keep an eye out for them.

"I'm going to send Max Redwood out there with you guys, ok – he'll be flying high above, keeping a lookout for any witches. Now, when you guys arrive at Jacks Point, somebody will be there waiting for you. She's an old lighthouse lady called Jennie – be nice to her because she's my old lover. She won't know you guys, but she knows Max very well. Once she sees little Max, she'll be nice to all of you, I promise."

Leon nodded to Sasha like a soldier, he knew exactly what he had to do, and he was ready to crack on with the mission.

It was around this time that I started to realise how Tigerlips seemed to be more of an open-hearted character, while Leon was more like a closed book; it takes all kinds I guess.

So, the time had come for the gang to split up. It was almost time for the twins to go. Leon wanted to check the oil level on his motorbike first.

Betty's jet powered rocket board provided some help for the rest of the gang – that board was our ticket back to London. This is what happened: Betty placed the board directly underneath The Fuzz Cat's ice cream van and clicked her fingers. The ironing board quickly changed shape, transforming itself into a huge surfboard. It hovered obediently while it awaited further instructions from Betty.

As soon as it was in the perfect position, Betty ordered the board to clamp itself firmly to the underbelly of the ice cream van. It wouldn't move at all now; it was locked in position.

The rocket board was now ready to carry the whole ice cream van back to London. It was easily powerful enough to carry the van with all of us on board. Driving the van back through Italy and France would have been a real drag. We didn't have time for a long drive through the mountains – there was too much to do.

We all piled into the van and flew far away from Sasha's coffee bar. Looking out the back window I saw Max and The Paradox Twins zoom off in the opposite direction. Tigerlips blew a kiss to Kelly Ann, and she quickly blew one back to him. The Fuzz Cats and I couldn't stop giggling.

Then Betty spoke up, "Oh I say, Wham Bam Kelly Ann, she's got the hots for the Tiger Man," we all laughed as Kelly Ann turned red.

"Oh, shut up," she said, as she quietly sniggered. She had a massive smile on her face, she was blushing. She was falling in love.

I suddenly felt the ice cream van pick up speed as it climbed high above the mountains. The jet-powered rocket board was coping with the load – no worries there. Our journey back to London was swift and smooth.

CHAPTER 18
WORK YOUR MAGIC, BETTY

We got back to Betty's laundrette around four in the morning. The neighbourhood was awfully quiet, but not for long. We drove down the secret winding tunnel and parked the ice cream van just where the spinner usually parks. As we climbed out of the van, Sasha told Betty that he wanted the ice cream van turned into a helicopter. Betty raised her eyebrows for two seconds, then she went straight to work on making this transformation a successful one.

She needed to make a pair of wings, so she decided to smash up her Spitfire fridge and gas cooker. Betty used an old hammer on the Spitfire fridge, while Penelope Jones boxed the living daylights out of the Spitfire gas cooker. They bashed away like a couple of nutters.

Betty quickly decided to take the whole project up on to the main street, parking the van right in front of the laundrette.

It was still very early in the morning, maybe five a.m. My goodness, we made so much noise. Lots of sleepy cranky people shouted out their windows telling us to shut up; some neighbours even threatened to call the police. I quickly ran over and apologised to them explaining that the ice cream van is an important part of an art exhibition, and it had to be finished before midday because it was going on parade. I hate telling lies, but that was much easier than saying thousands of horrible witches will be coming to attack us soon, and we need to be ready for them.

That was the unfortunate truth. Roaring Meg and all her mini witches were coming soon – there was no doubt about that. We were in a jam and we had to move fast. There was a very good reason why Sasha wanted the van turned into a helicopter; it will all make sense soon.

It was now time for the wings to be welded on. The Fuzz Cats helped Betty hold them in position while she welded away.

Penelope Jones was very excited about all this. She danced under all the splashy sparks as Betty welded. Being a ghost she could get as close as she wanted; all the sparks just showered right through her. Most things went through Penelope, but she could touch things if she wanted to. The old wrinkly boxer suddenly spoke up,

"Oh I say, this is just the kind of treat I've been hoping for, a nice sizzling hot shower. If only I had some mega hot volcanic lava for shampoo."

Penelope's silliness made me smile.

Attaching the wings was quite a task, but sweaty Betty never stopped working until the job was done – she was a trooper.

As soon as the wings were on, Betty went straight to work on making the helicopter engine. Sasha wanted the Titanic propeller to be the new helicopter blades; it was a pretty good idea. I will get back to the helicopter project in just a moment.

I took a break from watching the guys and went back down to the secret hideout cave, where Sasha and Kelly Ann were snooping around. Kelly Ann was intrigued by Betty's turbo-powered nitro-rocket roller skates – they looked fun and dangerous. She studied them with excited eyes. It was obvious she wanted to give them a try.

I was really interested in having a go on Betty's dinosaur-teeth skateboard. I wanted to find a big hill and give it a good test run, but there was no time for that. Sasha spent his minutes sorting through Betty's old jet-powered rocket boards – he was looking for a good one.

"Hey Sasha," I said.

"I reckon Meg must be getting close to releasing all those witches by now. What do you think?"

"Yes, not long now, honey." he said. "We need to be absolutely ready – that's all that matters."

I agreed, as I slipped Betty's skateboard under my arm, then I went back up to the street. I wasn't stealing it; I was just borrowing it for a while.

Back up on the street, Betty was halfway towards creating a magnificent helicopter engine. A big bulk of the work was already done because Betty had been working on creating a fantastic deluxe washing machine that spun at unnatural speeds. Her original plan was to make a machine that cleaned, washed, dried, and ironed clothes in under five minutes. That was the original plan, but now her half-built turbo deluxe washing machine had a new destiny. She immediately got busy with her tools and converted it into a high-performance helicopter engine. After half an hour of tinkering, she got The Fuzz Cats to fetch the Titanic propeller; everything was slowly coming together.

Betty was a tenacious mechanic. She worked hard and fast like a little ant. I was getting pretty excited about this project.

Well, let me tell you something – that big old Titanic propeller was the cherry on top.

The SUPERSONIC HELICOPTER ICE CREAM VAN was completely futuristic!

A proper chopper!

Betty put it all together like a genius, and she really appreciated all the help she got from The Fuzz Cats; they did all the heavy lifting.

Betty bolted everything down properly. My goodness, the new engine looked bold and beefy.

Advanced mechanics is, without a doubt, Betty's area of expertise; avant-garde machinery is her forte.

I suggested that maybe it would be a wise move to give the ice cream van's normal engine a quick check over. Betty and the Cats agreed. We all got busy changing the oil, replacing the spark plugs, and changing all the filters, then Betty gave it a sweet little tune-up, making sure it ran nice and smooth.

Then we checked over the helicopter engine. Everything looked set and ready, so Betty started it up. Sweet chilli peppers, it ran like a dream. It purred loudly, sounding keen and eager to make its maiden voyage. As the Titanic propeller picked up more speed, it got louder and louder, it soon created a swirl of wild wind, blowing newspapers and loose litter all around the neighbourhood. The unique loud sound of the new helicopter engine caught the attention of Sasha and Kelly Ann. They soon came up to the street to check out and admire Betty's magnificent work.

It was too early in the day to have such a loud engine running, so Sasha instructed Betty to switch it off.

When the Titanic propeller finally came to a halt, we heard a weird distant buzzing sound. At first, we thought there was something up with the engine. How wrong we were. The sound grew louder and louder. It came from far away but slowly grew in volume; it was a creepy jittering type of sound. At first, we thought it was a swarm of bees, but as the noise got closer we wised up to what it really was, it sounded more like a multitude of crazy giggles coming from the bellies of wild goblins.

"Is that what I think it is?" said Fuzz Cat Sam.

"I think so," replied Sasha.

The mini witches were close now.

Then Penelope Jones spoke up, "Oh, my goodness, this is it! This is fantastic!" We all looked at her in disbelief. "I mean, it's terrible. It's awful – let's make a sharp exit." Penelope was ready to fight, she was getting a dose of her 'old boxers adrenaline rush.' No doubt it was triggered from all the danger that was coming our way.

I suddenly noticed that Kelly Ann had already put the nitro-powered rocket skates on and was ready to give them a go. I was more than happy to have a go on the dinosaur-teeth skateboard. It was going to be a crazy morning in London Town, that was for sure. The witches had now arrived! Yikes, the time had come for the next stage of Sasha's master plan. We needed to get ourselves over to Camden Town as quick as possible.

CHAPTER 19
SOMETHING'S GOING DOWN, IN CAMDEN TOWN

I was blown away by what I saw when I looked up into the blue morning sky – thousands of green snotty nosed witches all staring down at us. Roaring Meg had finally set them free, and these witches were livid, baby.

They badly wanted to get their revenge on Sasha. They knew he was the one responsible for trapping them in that marble prison so many years ago.

Roaring Meg told the witches to go straight to Betty's laundrette and wipe the whole gang out, by whatever means necessary.

There were so many of them, but Meg was nowhere to be seen; her mind was pretty twisted and messed up. I reckon she stayed up on the moon knocking back bottles of whiskey. She had all her witches to do her dirty work now – and they were filled with blind rage.

I will never forget their faces. They looked angry, but they also looked old and knackered and lonely. I remember fearing them, but I also remember feeling sorry for them. They were like old zombies coming out of the graveyard, ready to have one last swing at trying to take over the world, they looked way past their prime; it was a bit sad really.

The Fuzz Cats quickly jumped back into the ice cream van. "Stick to the plan!" shouted Sasha. Fuzz Cat George popped his head out the window.

"Aye-aye, captain," was all he said, then the ice cream van drove off using Portobello Road for a runway. It sped off and flew up into the sky like a dream. It was a funny sight to see. The Titanic propeller and beefy helicopter engine worked in perfect harmony, the spitfire wings looked pretty cool too.

"Stick to the master plan, Kelly Ann!" shouted Sasha.

"Okey-dokey, daddio, see you in Camden Town," she said.

Sasha wanted all of us to get over to Camden Town as soon as we possibly could. This was the location for the next part of his fantastic master plan. Sasha was always one step ahead, thank goodness.

I stayed close to Kelly Ann. She roller-skated down the street while I skateboarded alongside her. Betty and Sasha were about to fly off on a couple of jet-powered rocket boards. Sasha had a good fast one now, but Betty's was faster.

"Oh, hang on a minute," said Betty. "I must water my dragon-fire daffodil. I'll be back in a jiffy." She quickly jumped off her board and ran back into the laundrette.

"For goodness sake, Betty! Hurry up!" shouted Sasha. Betty quickly watered her weird plant, ran back out, hopped up on her board, and flew over to where Sasha was waiting for her.

Penelope Jones flew above Kelly Ann and myself. Like a brave rugged angel, she dashed out in front of us searching for battle. She wanted to take on all the witches by herself; she had the spirit of a bold Viking. We didn't need to look too hard because the witches were flippin' everywhere!

"Here they come!" shouted Kelly Ann. I looked up to the sky and felt horrified. There were at least ten thousand witches staring down at us, a huge green cloud of witchy weirdos blocking out the morning sun.

They started to make their attack.

"Quick, follow me!" Kelly Ann roller-skated awfully fast. I did my best to keep up.

I was very impressed with Penelope. She distracted the witches terribly well; they all chased her instead of us. She took them off in a completely different direction, nice one, Penelope. This gave Kelly Ann and myself a good chance to make our escape. Sasha and Betty zoomed off in a completely different direction as well; they'd get to Camden soon enough. They flew their rocket boards down through the underground train tunnels; a dangerous choice but hard for the witches to follow.

I was skateboarding as fast as I could when Kelly

Ann suddenly reached out and grabbed my hand. I almost fell off, but I just about managed to retain my balance, then I watched Kelly Ann crouch down to activate the nitro-rockets attached to her roller skates. My goodness, as soon as she hit that button we took off like a Ducati motorbike.

I still have no idea how I stayed on that skateboard – it must have been the purple magic in my bloodstream looking after me. We swished our way up to the top of Portobello Road in under sixty seconds, then we killed it along the main drag, overtaking taxis, buses and cars all the way up to Marble Arch. We then shot over to Camden Town. Cutting through all the traffic was great fun, but the witches weren't giving up; they stuck to us like a bad habit.

It was such a busy morning when we arrived in Camden. There were people shopping everywhere, then the witches started to arrive.

Kelly Ann wanted to make a quick pit stop at her Dutch barge to pick up her saxophone. She was in and out like a flash, making her barge rock about on the still waters of the canal, then she played that sax with all her heart.

The sound of the saxophone was like a police siren warning people to get out of the way as we came tearing through the crowded streets. We had several witches chasing behind us now.

The Fuzz Cats had secretly arrived in Camden too,

they were getting ready to follow the next step of Sasha's master plan.

Kelly Ann and I skated along the canal foot path, we had a couple of witches on our tail, when the coolest thing happened.

Out of nowhere, one of The Fuzz Cats jumped out from behind a wall and grabbed the two witches with ease – it was Fuzz Cat Brian.

We stopped and watched what he did next. Brian had both the witches trapped under his arms in a double headlock. They wiggled about like freshly caught fish, but they were no match for Brian's electric strength. He went ahead and did something that I'd never seen before – he gave the two witches a big electric squeeze called a HUG-ZAP!

It's very straightforward and very effective. When Brian hugged the witches, thousands upon thousands of electric sparks came blasting out from his ears, making him glow up like he had a million light bulbs under his skin. This 'Fuzz Cat formula' successfully electrocuted the witches into a forty-eight hour coma.

"See ya later," was all Brian said, as the two witches fell to the ground.

Kelly Ann and I watched with vivid curiosity; this was a mesmerizing act. Brian knocked the witches out cold, then Fuzz Cat Bruce came along to give a helping hand. Both these cool cats carried the witches back to the ice cream van and laid them down in the back.

This hug-zap approach was Sasha's idea – we had to honour his request about using no violence. None of the witches got killed; we just put them all to sleep instead. This was all part of the plan.

That day in Camden Town turned out to be an electric master blaster. The Fuzz Cats dished out thousands of hug-zaps; they had the whole area secured. They must have spent maybe six hours catching and hug-zapping as many witches as they possibly could, the volume of sleeping witches piled up fast.

Kelly Ann's saxophone playing attracted the attention of many witches, but it also caught the attention of her old age pensioner friends – the ones who like to race in their electric-powered motor scooters. Well, they all lived in a retirement home just five minutes away from Camden Lock. After hearing the familiar sound of Kelly Ann's saxophone, twenty of Kelly Ann's wrinkly old friends turned up on their scooters, to help catch more witches.

These old age scooter pensioners were originally from the north of England. They hailed from a place called Hull, and they called themselves the 'Hull's Angels'. They helped trap lots of witches with their unique kung-fu knitting skills. Kelly Ann had taught them well. Many times on that day The Fuzz Cats hug-zapped a witch who'd been completely tied up with knitting wool. This was, of course, the skilful work of The Hull's Angels.

We soon ran into a small problem – there was nowhere left to store the sleeping witches.

The ice cream van got filled up in no time, and we stuffed well over a thousand witches into Kelly Ann's Dutch barge; that was my job.

I've got to be honest – I didn't like handling the witches. They gave me the heebie jeebies. They were light and brittle, fragile and stinky, and if I squeezed one too hard her bones crunched, and sometimes they snapped in half. They made me feel very uncomfortable.

Sasha and Betty were very busy in the skies above – I will tell you what they got up to in a moment. It was a very mad and hectic day. Thousands of witches chased Kelly Ann, Betty, Sasha, and Penelope. The Fuzz Cats kept bringing more and more unconscious witches to me, but I had nowhere to put them.

The Hull's Angels made excellent woolly booby traps. They looked like giant spider webs – they were very effective. The whole team that day had a good formula: Kelly Ann slyly drew the witches into the nets, and once they got tangled up, five or six of The Hull's Angels jumped on them and tied them up good, kung-fu style. It was like catching big ugly Dragonflies, and soon after that, one of The Fuzz Cats swung by to hug-zap the living daylights out of them. Sweet teamwork in motion, baby.

After every hug-zap was carried out, The Fuzz Cat always said, "See ya later!"

Penelope Jones helped out a great deal too. I remember her calling my name out as she hovered high above the canal, she had something she wanted to show me.

"Hey Louise, check this out, I've just invented a brand new sport. It's called SKY-BOXING!" She then hid inside a weeping willow tree and waited for about five seconds, and when the next green snotty-nosed witch flew past, Penelope jumped out and gave her the biggest swooping left upper-cut power punch ever, this was immediately followed by an ultra-sonic sledgehammer right hook. This double punch combination technique immediately knocked the poor witch out cold. The witch quickly fell to the ground and soon got hug zapped by Fuzz Cat George. Penelope did this dirty work behind Sasha's back, cheeky old girl, she loved her boxing. Lots of witches flew after her, but she kept escaping by flying through solid brick walls. The witches had no idea she was a ghost, they tried to follow, but they crashed every time. They'd be on the floor in a dizzy daze, and after maybe ten seconds, a Fuzz Cat came along and hug-zapped them to sleep.

"See ya later!"

The Fuzz Cats were having a field day. They just kept bringing more and more sleeping witches to me, and I still didn't have a clue where to put them. I will tell you more about that in a minute.

Sasha and Betty were just about coping in the skies

above; they had two forms of defence. Betty had a huge bag of exploding bangers and meatballs, and Sasha had a big pocket that was filled with flying saucer sweets. Sasha's sweets weren't normal flying saucer sweets. They contained a powder which had fresh garlic mixed with purple magic, so every time a witch got close to him, he quickly put a flying saucer sweet in his mouth, huffed a massive puff, and a stinky mass of garlic breath knocked the witches out cold. They soon fell to the ground and got hug-zapped by the nearest Fuzz Cat.

I think being trapped in the marble prison for such a long time made these witches rusty flyers; they flew like old ladies with bad eyesight. They were easily over a thousand years old; they probably needed glasses.

The exploding bangers and meatballs worked exceptionally well. Betty knocked out many witches with these magic meaty snacks. The meat blew-up in their face, turned to dust, and the unlucky witch fell asleep in mid-air, she then slowly drifted down to the ground, like a snowflake, and soon enough got zing fired by another Fuzz Cat Hug-Zap.

By the end of the afternoon, I was completely knackered. We now had a mega huge pile of sleeping witches stacked up beside Kelly Ann's Dutch barge.

Looking over to the other side of the canal, I suddenly noticed a huge construction site. It looked like a new block of apartments were being made, but it was no way finished. The building stood naked, looking like a huge stack of concrete shelves.

I suggested to Sasha that we use the building to store all the remaining witches. Sasha took one look over and said, "Yes, that's the ticket."

We all got busy transporting the sleeping witches over to the new building. The Fuzz Cats did most of the lifting and shifting; the new building got filled up in no time. Then I looked up to the sky with shock and horror, more and more witches kept coming. MAMMA MIA! This was all becoming a bit too crazy, but on a positive note, we WERE making progress. We were thinning the number of witches down all right. We just had to persevere – keep on keeping on – and keep sticking to Sasha's plan.

Then, straight out of the blue, Sasha shouted over to me. He was desperate to get my attention.

"Hey, Louise!" he said.

"Yes, Sasha," I answered. I was still standing on Kelly Ann's Dutch barge handing more yukky witches down to The Fuzz Cats, when Sasha suddenly pulled something out of his pocket and threw it over to me.

"Catch!" he shouted. He threw something that looked like an acorn, but when I caught it, I realised it was a small piece of pure purple magic. Sasha quickly shouted something out, just before I caught it.

"Get ready for another heart visit, Louise. Ha ha!" Holy Wagon Wheels!

I spontaneously disappeared from Camden Town

and got ZIP-SLASHED at the speed of light over to New Zealand. I was suddenly back inside Max Redwood's little heart.

Here we go again.

CHAPTER 20
A QUICK PIT-STOP AT JENNIE'S

Sasha wanted me to check up on the current situation with Max Redwood and The Paradox Twins. I must say, looking out onto the world through the eyes of Max Redwood was quite interesting, and I was very happy to be away from all those yukky witches. We flew way up at the top of the sky, about a mile above the Pacific Ocean. I saw New Zealand way over yonder. To be honest, I thought The Paradox Twins would be on their way back by now, because so much time had gone by. That's when Max told me about their unscheduled visit to Cuba; Leon went to Havana to pick up a box of Cuban cigars.

As I looked down, I saw half a dozen witches chasing the twins. Oh dear, more snot-faced twits. Four of them were chasing Leon's flying motorbike, and the other two were chasing Tigerlips in the spinner speedboat.

We were flying over the South Island now, getting closer and closer to Jack's Point. I saw the lighthouse down on the beach and that's when Max began his descent. The lighthouse stood all alone right at the tip of the shore. It was big and white, and it flashed a purple light.

"That's got to be Jack's Point, just over there," I said.

"Yes, it is," whistled Max.

Excellent, this heart visit was much easier than the last one – more space in Max's heart and no heavy lifting, bonus.

Looking down at the lighthouse, I saw a woman come out from the main door. She was in a wheelchair, and she was holding something that looked like a magic wand.

I watched her raise both her hands as she threw out a huge thunderous spell, and all six witches instantly fell to the ground. Like autumn leaves, they landed lightly on the beach.

Leon immediately followed them down, landing his IRON JOHN motorbike gracefully on the sand. It was a nice beach, very wide and flat. Leon slowly pulled up and parked close to the lighthouse. He stayed on his bike, lit a cigar and just chilled for a few minutes.

Tigerlips approached the lighthouse next. He cruised through the choppy waves at top speed. Pushing the 'turbo-wash' button just at the right time was crucial; thankfully, Tigerlips was a natural. He transformed the spinner back into a car just as it crossed over from sea to land. It was a cool transformation to watch.

Max decided to land on Leon's shoulder – a gutsy move, I thought.

I was intrigued by Jennie, the mysterious lighthouse lady. She looked old and jaded but very wise. As we got closer, I saw that she had no legs; instead, she had a big green fin with lots of shiny scales. Great Scott, she was a mermaid – a very old one, maybe a pensioner.

"Greetings, we've come on behalf of Sonic Sasha," said Tigerlips, he bowed his head a little, to show some respect and thanks to Jennie for taking care of the six witches.

"We're here to collect his supply of purple magic," he said.

Jennie looked rigid, stubborn and lonely. She had been Sasha's lover for a long time; I think she still loved him. Max told me Sasha and Jennie were deeply in love with each other many years ago, old flames.

Jennie is the mother of Betty and Kelly Ann, but things got so difficult for Jennie and Sasha – their relationship was too intense. It's hard for a wizard and a mermaid to find a natural feeling of compatibility. I guess sometimes things just aren't meant to be, and people just need to let go of each other and move on, but that's not an easy thing to do when you're deeply in love. This seemed to be the case with Jennie.

Taking a good long look, I noticed that Jennie's wheelchair was quite unique. It looked like a big fish tank on wheels. The bottom half of her body had to be kept under water all the time; it was vital that she kept her fin wet, twenty-four seven.

"Sasha's purple magic!" she said, with a snappy tone. I'm glad you guys have finally come to collect it."

Jennie looked exhausted, but her bold eyes glistened with undeniable joy when Sasha's name was mentioned. She still had strong feelings for him – the eyes never lie.

"I've been guarding his flipping purple magic for too long," she said. Jennie swivelled around in her wheelchair and reached for something that was tucked just behind the front door. It was Sasha's purple magic supply, stored in an old brown leather suitcase.

Jennie dragged it out onto the front porch and threw it down on the old wooden decking in front of her. She must have known we were coming. Poor Jennie, she looked very upset.

"Here, take it away," she said.

The case popped open, and I saw the purple magic inside. It looked like a massive bar of transparent purple soap; it glowed with a cool mellow light.

"That's all of it." Jennie spoke with an air of relief in her voice. She was glad to see it go.

Leon got off his motorbike and walked over to pick it up. That's when Max and I flew off and landed on Tigerlip's shoulder.

Leon bent down, closed the case, and slowly picked it up right in front of the old spinster mermaid. Jennie was completely unafraid to stare at the wolf-man, she took a good long look at him, gazing like a confident child.

"I say, you're a funny-looking fellow, aren't you?" Leon tried to be polite, but he wasn't very good at using manners. He stared at Jennie for ten seconds, took a big lug on his cigar, blew the smoke out and slowly walked back to his motorbike, then he carefully placed the leather suitcase in his sidecar – he strapped it in good with the seatbelt.

Then Tigerlips jumped out of the spinner and ran over to pick up the six unconscious witches lying on the beach. We flew over, and hovered just above him while he threw the witches over his shoulder, they were light and flimsy like long streaks of seaweed, he soon chucked them onto the red chesterfield sofa in the back of the spinner. It was a snug fit. That chesterfield sofa needed wiping down, it still had dried up strawberry jam stains and sticky coffee spillings all over it, left by the fat couple back in London. The sharp nose of Tigerlips picked up the sweet scent of the jam, he sniffed it out and decided to lick it all off, the jam and the coffee, crazy cat.

Max and I wanted to feel the energy of the purple magic, so we flew over and landed on the handlebars of Leon's motorbike, but the wolf-man was still busy puffing on his cigar, and Max doesn't like cigar smoke, so we decided to swish over and say hi to Jennie. Max landed on her shoulder.

"Oh, my goodness! I remember you." Jennie's voice suddenly became lighter and happier.

"Hello, my old friend."

Jennie and Max were good pals back in the day. She turned her head to Max and whispered something in his ear. I heard every word, of course.

"Tell Sasha I will always love him, and let him know that I can be found deep in the ocean, if he ever needs me."

This wonderful mermaid-woman still had a universe of love in her heart, and it was all for Sasha. Sometimes it's very hard to just switch love off, this seemed to be the case with Jennie.

She was awfully pleased to see Max, but deep down inside, she seemed to be very tired and uninspired. She looked unloved, and this made my heart sad. She gently took Max off her shoulder and held him in her hand, Max quickly perched himself up on her wrinkly old index finger. Jennie leaned forward and gave Max a little kiss on the side of his head.

"I'll be on my way now," she whispered. "I am no longer needed here. At last, I can go back to the ocean, back home, to where I belong."

Jennie suddenly took out her magic wand and proceeded to sprinkle a glittery spell all over herself. Lots of little white pieces of shiny stardust poured out from the magic wand like sparkling water coming out of a shower head. The sparks looked like bright miniature snowflakes. When the spell was cast, Jennie tossed the wand over to Tigerlips; he caught it with ease.

"Give this wand to my daughter, Kelly Ann." That was all she said, then Max and I suddenly felt a shift of energy in the air, so we quickly flew back over to Leon and stood on the headlamp of his motorbike.

Jennie suddenly drifted upwards and started floating over her wheelchair. She hovered about ten meters above us. Lots of water dripped from her beautiful mermaid fin, after a few more drippy seconds she started spinning around and around, gradually turning into a colourful twisting gust of wind.

We watched her gracefully waltz her way through the sky as she drifted back over towards the ocean. We gazed on with wonder as she gently flew further and further out to sea, then she suddenly turned back into a young, beautiful mermaid – this was awesome. She splashed into the sea like a dolphin and that was it, she was gone forever, but wait – after five more seconds, her mermaid fin popped up and wiggled a little wave. That was her way of saying goodbye, I guess.

Sweet heavens above, that was pretty to watch. She swam off into another world, free at last.

"Now, there's something you don't see every day," said Tigerlips. He examined the magic wand and cheekily started using it as a toothpick, removing dried bits of old sticky strawberry jam, then he safely tucked it away in his leather jacket.

Max suddenly moved very fast without any warning, he jumped up from the headlamp and started flapping and hovering directly in front of Leon's face. The cheeky robin purposely used the tips of his wings to flick all the hot ashes away from Leon's cigar, he did this for a few seconds until the cigar was completely extinguished. Leon was not impressed with this, so he quickly raised his right hand and caught Max in mid-air. Leon stared at Max for the longest moment.

In a scratchy sand paper voice the wold man said three words, "DON'T DO THAT!"

Max gulped, then he whistled out a short bossy tune, and Leon released him from his grip. Leon was a scary road warrior, but I liked him. Soon after that, both The Paradox Twins started their engines. It was time for us to head back to England.

The next part of the plan was to meet up with the rest of the guys, back in London. A rendezvous at Highgate Cemetery had been arranged.

Now, to avoid being seen by any more disgusting witches, we decided to fly under the world instead of around it. It was safer and quicker to fly back over the South Pole, then Africa, Spain, and France, then glide over Brighton, and head straight for London.

Leon flew above while Tigerlips sped through land and sea below. Max continued flying at a much higher altitude – it was the best place to be when looking out for witches. Tigerlips sped the spinner speedboat at top speed. As we journeyed north, he cruised through the choppy waves up the west coast of Africa.

This was the quickest route back to England. We hoped and prayed for a witch-free journey, and that's exactly what we got. Get in!

CHAPTER 21
RENDEZVOUS AT THE
GRAVEYARD

As soon as we arrived at Highgate Cemetery, my heart visit was over. I looked like a ghostly cloud of mist when Max breathed me out, but after five seconds, I turned back to my normal 'weird' self, ha ha.

It was kind of cool being back at Highgate Cemetery. I liked being back at the exact same spot where Betty saved my life, but this time all the gang were there. Nobody disturbed us in the graveyard; it was a good secret place to meet. There were a few ghosts lurking about, but they caused no bother. They just wanted to chat with Penelope Jones – she's a celebrity ghost.

I walked over and helped Tigerlips take the six witches out of the spinner, we put them straight in the back of the ice cream van. I was very impressed with all the news I heard from the gang. They had all performed exceptionally well, not to forget the Hull's Angels – they did a great job too. No doubt they were back at their retirement home, probably knitting scarves and jumpers. The whole operation in Camden Town was a complete success, a fantastic team effort.

Sasha was right when he said, 'TEAMWORK MAKES THE DREAM WORK'.

So, what was next? We now had a great deal of sleeping witches to move – they were stored everywhere, let's see.

Betty's laundrette in Portobello was filled with sleeping witches, her secret underground cave was full up, Kelly Ann's Dutch barge was completely full up, the new unfinished block of flats on the construction site by the canal was full up, and we now had six fresh ones in the back of The Fuzz Cat's ice cream van.

"We still have lots of sleeping witches left over," said Sasha.

"Really? Where are they?" I asked.

Sasha had a cheeky grin on his face.

"Well, I couldn't think of anywhere else to put them, so I dumped the remaining witches in the middle of Lord's Cricket Ground. There's a huge pile of about three thousand green grotty stinkers sleeping on the cricket square right now," Sasha laughed.

We were all quite pleased and happy with ourselves. It had been a hard day's night, or a hard night's day, something like that, I think I had a dose of jet-lag, it was a lot of hard work; that's what I'm trying to say, everything was moving in the right direction, and that was all that really mattered.

"What about Roaring Meg?" I asked. "What's she up to?"

"I think she's still up on the moon," said Sasha. "She's probably watching TV and drinking her whiskey."

"Oh dear," I said.

Sasha continued, "She's gotten worse over the years, you know, she's definitely losing her marbles." Sasha put his hands up to his face. "Poor Meg," he said.

It was around eight thirty in the evening, and we were all slowly beginning to unwind. Leon built a nice little campfire, and we all gathered around it. Kelly Ann suddenly decided that she wanted to check out the purple magic, so she took it out from Leon's flying motorbike side-car and opened the case right up, it had a great scent to it – like fresh lavender. A calm feeling of peace oozed out from it, helping all of us relax. It also made the campfire's flames roar up in glory. In that fleeting moment, I saw the light of the flickering flames dance all over the faces of everyone sitting around the fire. Such extraordinary faces, all of them. I was hanging out with some ubercool outsiders.

Max Redwood was happy to be sitting back on Sasha's shoulder. I also noticed how Tigerlips and Kelly Ann had gotten themselves into a nice laid back relaxing cuddle, they were all smooched up together, completely chilled out like a couple on a sofa, watching a movie, only they were watching the fire.

Tigerlips took Jennie's magic wand out from his coat pocket and gave it straight to his new girlfriend.

Her face lit up with excitement, then Betty put her arm around me. She was so kind. She made me feel rich and blessed; I felt like a genuine member of the gang now.

Fuzz Cat Sam got up and fetched his small ukulele from the ice cream van, and once he tuned all the strings, he started strumming and singing some mellow songs to us. His singing made a nice atmosphere, his voice was lovely, very soothing. He seemed to purr and meow while he sang, what a sweet delightful groovy weirdo.

We all slowly slipped into a nice chilled-out state of mind, then Leon lit a cigar, and Betty had a little smoke on her pipe.

"You really ought to quit that nasty habit, you know," said Sasha. He was not pleased to see his daughter smoking.

"Yes, it's silly to smoke," said Penelope. She was sitting right in the middle of the fire.

My attention suddenly got drawn to another Fuzz Cat. I heard lots of sizzle popping sounds come from Fuzz Cat Bruce. He'd fallen into a deep sleep, and in his dream, he was still dishing out lots of hug-zaps to numerous witches. We all laughed as he wiggled about on the ground. He looked silly, but he was entertaining to watch. Tigerlips reached over to wake him with just a gentle nudge.

"Wakey wakey, it's only a dream, old boy," he said.

Fuzz Cat Bruce immediately woke up and jumped right out of his skin. He thought Tigerlips was a witch, so he grabbed him fast and gave him the biggest hug-zap ever! It made such a loud crackly noise. Sparks flew everywhere as Tigerlips got shocked right down to his bones.

"Ahhhhhhhhh! Stop it, it tickles," he shouted. Being one-third electric eel, Tigerlips quite enjoyed the extra voltage. Bruce was fully awake now.

"Oh, my goodness, I'm terribly sorry about that." All the hair on Tigerlip's head smoked and crackled, it was extra frizzy now.

"No problem, mate," said Tigerlips. "It felt quite good, actually." Tigerlips was now in a happy daze.

Kelly Ann wanted to comfort her new boyfriend so she reached out to put her arm around him, but she got the biggest shock of her life! She got fire-snapped by all the electricity and flew up high into the sky. On her way back down, she landed in a tree and woke up a sleeping owl, everybody laughed.

Soon after that, everyone went quiet for a few minutes, but the silence soon got broken by Penelope Jones – she had a question for us.

"I've been wondering, guys – how the heck are we going to get all these sleeping witches transported over to Hudson Bay?"

"That is what you want? Right, Sasha?"

"Yes, of course," he said. "That's the next part of the masterplan. I want all the witches loaded up onto the Titanic."

It was a very strange masterplan. I'm glad Sasha knew what he was doing, because the rest of the gang didn't seem to have a clue.

We had a slight little issue now, none of us, including Sasha, knew how we were going to get all the witches transported over to Canada, this problem was a tricky one to figure out. It was the only part of Sasha's masterplan that needed some creative input. Silence took over as we all stared into the fire, everybody's imagination went to work as we quietly brainstormed.

"We need to get every single witch over to the Titanic in Hudson Bay? Well, how are we going to do that?" asked Tigerlips.

"I have an idea!" I announced. "Not so long ago, we flew over a travelling circus in Regent's Park. They were setting up a huge circus tent. Well, maybe we could borrow their tent for a while. It definitely looked big enough to carry a humongous pile of sleeping witches."

"Bingo! That should do it," said Betty.

"I think it's a great idea," said Kelly Ann.

"Yes, I like it too," said Sasha.

All the gang agreed. Yes!

Although we were all such different individuals, there was one thing we all had in common that night – we were all completely starving. So, Fuzz Cat Brian and Betty walked up to Highgate Village and grabbed a dozen portions of fish and chips, and chicken pies too.

They soon returned and we all got stuck in. For ten seconds I started thinking about my dad, the strong smell of the fish and chips made me think about him and his cheeky character, I love my old man so much; then my quiet nostalgic thoughts got wildly interrupted by Betty's loud voice.

"I need more ketchup on my chips," she said, so I handed a couple of ketchup sachets to her, and that's when I saw Leon's fangs grow bigger. His vampire desires were starting to tingle, then he spoke.

"I don't mind ketchup on my chips, but I much prefer some fresh human blood. Mmmmmm, much tastier."

"Hey, cut that out!" said Sasha.

Sasha understood Leon – he knew the wolf-man had a dark side. Leon shrugged his shoulders, then he looked right into my eyes.

"Nobody's perfect," he said. His icy blue eyes squinted a tiny sparkle, and for the first time ever I saw those cold eyes shine a warm light, he almost had a smile on his face. He was a funny old beast. It was good to see him finally loosening up. Deep down I think he was kind, very deep down.

Everyone became sleepy after their fish and chips, but nobody went to bed. We all just chilled for a while, and waited until after midnight before we got moving again; most of London would be asleep by then.

Around fifteen minutes after midnight Sasha stood

upright and said, "Ok, come on guys, up we get. We need to get moving now. There's a huge circus tent in Regent's Park calling out to us, I believe it wants to help us complete our mission."

Sasha's sharp eye suddenly caught my eye, so he gave me a quick snappy wink.

And off we went to Regent's Park.

CHAPTER 22
THE BUSY NIGHT SHIFT

The whole gang stayed together for this cheeky little mission. We just about managed to squeeze everyone into the ice cream van, including the six witches already stuffed in the back. We dropped them off at Lord's Cricket Ground first. The plan was that we DRIVE the van because the helicopter engine was too loud. We had to be subtle – the ice cream van's normal engine was smooth and quiet. It had a nice hush-hush sound, apart from second gear, second gear was a bit grindy. Arriving at Regent's Park, Sasha turned to us and said, "Ok, huddle up guys, this is a sneaky operation, ok. We need to be as quiet as mice, so stay sharp, be cool, and keep on your toes. It's going to be a long night." We all quietly shuffled out of the ice cream van and waited for further instructions from Sasha.

Nobody noticed how Tigerlips stayed back and lingered about inside the van. He was snooping around looking for ice cream when a little black box on the dashboard caught his attention, it had a big red switch.

"I wonder what that does?" he said. When he hit the switch, lots of loud childish lullaby music suddenly came bursting out of a big speaker from under the hood. Faster than a greyhound, Fuzz Cat George ran over and quickly switched it off.

"Come on, Tigerlips, man! Act professional!"

"Sorry, George," was all Tigerlips said, as he sniggered away.

Holy smoking bananas, I was blown away when I saw the size of the circus tent – it was ma-hoo-sive. It was the mothership of all tents. I had to tilt my head right back just so my eyes could take it all in; it was easily the biggest tent I'd ever seen.

"Ok, Listen," whispered Sasha. "We are not here to steal this tent, ok. We're just borrowing it for a while."

"Would that be a long while?" asked Kelly Ann, as she giggled. Then, Betty started to giggle, and that made Leon snigger, and that gave The Fuzz Cats the giggles; Tigerlips was already giggling. I tried so hard not to laugh that I ended up getting the hiccups. We all had the giggles now, and there was nothing we could do about it.

Sasha had the giggles too, so he decided to act fast; he quickly created a huge soundproof bubble for us to work in. This way, we wouldn't disturb the travelling circus people, who were sleeping over yonder in their gipsy caravans.

Sasha conducted many spells, but the best was still yet to come. That would be the Boombastic fantastic groovy Titanic spell. I will tell you more about that soon. Sonic Sasha was a tip-top wizard.

We quietly went to work on dismantling the circus tent, taking all the steel pegs out of the ground – this was easier said than done. They'd been whacked in good and hard; it took quite a while to wiggle them out. When we finally unpegged the last pin, we gave it our best shot to fold the tent up, but this drove us nuts, so we just scrunched it up instead. We quickly tied all the tent's ropes to the back of the ice cream van and got ready to make our getaway.

The ice cream van had a good strong tow bar at the back; it came in very handy, I must say. It was time to fly. George started up the fantastic helicopter engine, and the Titanic propeller spun like a magnificent fan; it was such a cool invention. Betty is a genius.

We all quickly hopped back into the van and swooped up into the sky. When the ice cream van touched Sasha's sound-proof bubble, it immediately popped and disappeared, like a normal soap bubble at bathtime.

We were on our way. We had to fly extra high now because we didn't want the tent to bump into any buildings below. This was just the beginning of our long night shift. It was time to collect all the sleeping witches; we had many stops to make. First up was Betty's place.

Arriving back in the Portobello area, we quickly landed in front of Betty's laundrette, opened the big tent up to the best of our ability, and got busy filling it up. We moved like ninja butterflies, silent but swift.

Holy Peter Pancakes. When I first walked into the laundrette, I was shocked to see what I saw – there were sleeping witches all over the place. Betty's laundrette was rammed-jammed from top to bottom. ALL the witches were still sleeping like babies, thank goodness. Green ugly goblin-babies, ha-ha. It looked like the aftermath of a huge witch party. They were everywhere, sprawled out on the floor, lying on top of the washing machines, slouching on the big long wooden benches, chilling in the little office in the back, and snoozing under the office desk. Everywhere you looked there were sleeping witches, so one by one, we took them outside and placed them in a pile, in the middle of the tent.

A few times during this operation, I stopped to take a good long look at some of these old green girlies. I got right up close and examined their faces. Sweet lord, they looked absolutely awful. Some only had one ear, some had no teeth, some only had one arm, some only had one eye, and the place where there once was a second eye was now just a small patch of green skin. Some had no hair – they just had these big bald green heads. They all looked battered and beaten up. I felt sad for these witches; none of them looked happy or healthy.

As soon as the laundrette was empty, the whole gang formed a chain-gang and brought all the witches up from the secret hideout cave below. I was at the end of the chain, so I got to see how Max Redwood and Penelope Jones kept busy organising the tent. They did something special with all the ropes; they somehow turned the huge tent into a huge giant sack. Penelope's plan was to make it look like a giant punch bag, she always found a way to bring the sport of boxing into the equation. We all started calling it the 'CIRCUS SACK'. Max and Penelope did a first-class job; all the witches were in position, bagged up nicely.

"Oh, I almost forgot," whispered Betty. "I've got some more witches stored around the corner, in my private lock-up."

Betty's private lock-up is a small garage workspace located under a bridge, in one of the arches beneath a busy train track, this was the place where she built the spinner, she also makes lots of freaky furniture down there, from old smashed up cars. She sells her freaky stuff in Portobello Market, every Saturday.

Kelly Ann and Tigerlips volunteered to pop over to the lock-up and collect the sleeping witches. They quickly hopped in the ice cream van and shot off around the corner, but they were gone for ages.

When they finally got back, they looked terribly smug and happy with themselves. My guess is they quickly threw the witches in the van and spent buckets of time kissing and snogging each other's faces off. They were a sweet couple, very odd-looking, but delightfully charming. They suited each other very well, opposites attract.

"Well, hello," whispered Betty, as she put her arm around her little sister.

"Someone looks very happy with themselves, don't they?" Kelly Ann's face turned red as she tried to keep her smile discreet.

Tigerlips tried to look innocent, but he had Kelly Ann's purple lipstick smeared all over his face.

We had lots of witches bundled together now; it was time to put the circus sack to the test. We all grabbed the thick rope that Max and Penelope had fixed up. The whole gang helped tie the bag up – stage one almost done.

Sasha quickly ordered The Paradox Twins to pop back into the laundrette to do a last-minute idiot check, just in case any witches had been overlooked. Leon found one – she was all cooped up inside one of the big tumble dryers, he quickly threw her into the circus sack, then we all hurried back into the van.

"Ok, all clear now," whispered Fuzz Cat George. And we were off, flying steady, slowly climbing up into the starry skies above. Max Redwood and Penelope Jones flew independently – they wanted to keep an eye on the circus sack below. It swung beneath us like a huge wrecking ball; it was working, the tow bar at the back of the ice cream van was mighty strong, thank goodness for that.

Everything looked good – the next stop was Camden Town. It was time to go back to Kelly Ann's Dutch barge on the canal and revisit the construction site; where thousands of sleeping witches were waiting for us.

We took care of that visit nice and quick. We had to be quick because it was around half three in the morning, and we wanted to get out of London before the rush hour. The ice cream van picked up all the Camden witches with absolute ease. Our plan was moving along nicely – so far, so good.

Betty's custom-made helicopter engine was solid, and the circus sack coped with all the weight, no problems there. It was made of thick canvas, very strong.

"One more stop to make," said Sasha. "Destination: Lord's Cricket Ground."

The ice cream van flew high above the streets of North London. We must have been a strange sight to look at. It's not every day you see a flying ice cream van with a huge sack of sleeping witches dangling underneath. Looking down, I saw a milkman doing his early morning round. He looked up to us in a state of complete shock, then he crashed his milk float into a lamp post. Oops-a-daisy, there was smashed glass and puddles of milk everywhere.

"I say, we're terribly sorry about that, old boy!" shouted Sasha.

"Don't cry over spilt milk," shouted Betty. We all giggled, then we flew on over to London Zoo. I can remember looking down at the giraffes, and seeing how they were looking back at us. I guess all the other animals were still sleeping. As soon as we arrived at Lord's Cricket Ground, we gently unfolded the circus sack and started loading up more witches. We had over ten thousand sleeping witches now, and another three thousand in front of us; we moved like cheeky foxes. We didn't want to be too rough with these old girls; it made sense to handle them with care. They were in a deep trance, a forty-eight-hour coma, but it was still very possible to wake them, and if just one witch woke up she'd, no doubt, go straight to work on waking all the others. That would have put us in a right pickle – the last thing we wanted was another hug-zap-athon. Imagine having to go through the whole Camden Town shebang one more time, no thank you Sir. It was wise to use a gentle approach, keep 'em sleepy, nice and easy does it.

An hour of lifting and shifting flew by, and we were all done. Every single witch had been successfully crammed into the circus sack; it was now time for the whole gang to put London behind us and fly over the Atlantic Ocean.

Sasha spoke up, "Hudson Bay, here we come."

All the gang felt quite pleased with themselves, except for the lonely wolf man. Leon was in an awfully stubborn mood – he made it quite clear that he didn't want to travel in the ice cream van anymore. He wanted to be sitting back in the driver's seat of his IRON JOHN flying motorbike. He told the gang that he was going to hop in a cab and head back to Highgate Cemetery, to pick up his bike. He briskly walked out of the cricket grounds and waved down a black taxi. I decided to tag along with him. Sasha knew we'd catch up soon enough.

Our ride in the black taxi was quite comical – I think the sight of Leon's fangs put the taxi driver under a lot of stress. With a shaky hand, he lit up a cigarette, and when he finished it, he lit his second cigarette with the first one. Leon sat in the back like a solid statue, he was completely relaxed as he puffed away on a fresh Cuban cigar, those cigars were so stinky! Leon truly has a very intimidating presence. He's not scared of anyone or anything, and nobody ever gives him any trouble, I feel quite safe when I'm with him, it's like being under the wing of a dragon.

I suddenly got the urge to turn around and look out the back window – and that's when I caught a glimpse of the ice cream van slowly taking off into the sky. The huge circus sack looked like a giant punch bag now – just like Penelope said it would.

Arriving back at the cemetery, we hopped out of the cab and walked over to pay the driver, but he zoomed off in a flash! Ha! Leon must have scared the living

Hoo-Bee-Doo-Bees out of him – the fact that he was taking us to the cemetery probably didn't help his nerves.

We quickly popped into the graveyard and fetched Leon's motorbike. It must've been around half five in the morning now; I always had to guess the time. Believe it or not, I still had my little shooting star watch on my wrist; it stopped working years ago but I could never throw it away, it was my lucky charm now, it reminded me so much of my dad. I continued wearing it for sentimental reasons.

Morning time was slowly coming into view. The sky was all fiery orange, and the rising sun looked beautiful. We took off quickly and flew west – it was time to catch up with the rest of the gang.

The purple magic was no longer in Leon's sidecar; it was safely tucked away in the back of the ice cream van. Our journey to Hudson Bay had finally begun. I was happy to stay with Leon. It was awfully loud sitting in the sidecar of IRON JOHN, but I kind of liked it. I pretended I was sitting in a Spitfire, flying over the English countryside under the morning sun was a real treat, the views were fantastic!

We caught up with the guys just as they were flying over Ireland. The circus sack swung wildly in the wind, but all the witches were fine, they were safely bagged up, sleeping the morning away. There was just one question I had in my mind, – What about Meg?

Where was Roaring Meg?

CHAPTER 23
A PUNCH-UP IN THE SKY

As you have probably come to realise, Sasha's master plan was indeed a very unorthodox operation. Meg's plan, however, was very simple. She wanted to wipe out the whole gang, brainwash billions of people, and take control over the world. Can you imagine that? Some crazy fool having the nerve to try and brainwash the entire human race? I mean, how would they do that? Sounds crazy right, but this was Meg's long-term plan.

There was just one thing she'd underestimated; and that was the sheer willpower and determination of our unique tenacious gang. When you have a gang who devotes all their strength and intelligence to teamwork, well, there's no telling what they can do. These guys worked together like a symphony of wonder, a synchronised unfolding of unbreakable greatness, and they always achieved their desired goal.

Meg must have wondered why none of the witches had flown back to the moon to report on their progress. She had no idea that her snoozing mini witch army was now being transported over the Atlantic Ocean in a giant sleeping bag, ha!

She searched high and low for her troops in London, but that turned out to be a waste of time; no doubt this filled her with more poisonous witch rage. Meg was still obsessed about getting her revenge on Sasha. Sasha knew Meg would find us – it was just a matter of time, but strangely enough, this is what Sasha wanted. He wanted Meg to follow us to Hudson Bay; this was all part of his genius plan.

Flying high in IRON JOHN, I looked out the window and saw Greenland under some passing clouds below. This indicated that we had now flown more than halfway over the Atlantic Ocean. We were now flying over the Labrador Sea, but I didn't see any dogs. Looking over to the ice cream van, I saw Kelly Ann staring out the window. She had a very serious look on her face; her psychic powers were twitching about inside. It was like her heart received a text message that quickly bubbled up to her brain.

She turned to the rest of the gang in the van and shouted at the top of her voice, "ROARING MEG IS CLOSE BY. I CAN FEEL HER PRESENCE. SHE'S COMING FOR THE WHOLE GANG!"

"No worries," said Sasha. He remained cool and calm, as usual. We were approaching Quebec now. Leon and I flew close behind, while Penelope and Max flew lower; they kept a sharp eye on the circus sack.

Looking over to the ice cream van once again, I saw Betty and Kelly Ann waving to us, so I smiled and waved back. Then, Betty held up a small scribbly sign that said, "LOOK OUT!"

That's when I looked in the motorbike's rear-view mirror and saw Roaring Meg on her black surfboard. She was racing towards us like a wild vulture; she looked really ticked off. She waved one fist in the air while her other fist was wrapped around a half-finished bottle of Jack Daniels. She was just about managing to keep her balance. She couldn't cast any evil spells because she was completely plastered – poor old Meg. She was up to her old tricks again – drinking and flying – silly old cow.

I looked over to the lonely wolf man and suddenly noticed that Leon's face had surprisingly become much hairier, and he was jolting about, acting funny, like he was having a sneeze attack. He crouched down and jittered around like he was shivering – something spooky was going on here. It all started to make sense when I saw the full moon shining its silver light down on us. Leon was turning into a werewolf – yikes. Deep down, I was quite glad about this because Meg was ultra-determined to kill and destroy us, and having a werewolf on our team gave us a higher chance of staying alive; that's how I saw it.

Meg suddenly came crashing into us. She jumped and landed on the backseat of the motorbike, dropping her bottle of whiskey she wrapped both her arms around Leon's head. She tried her very best to scratch his face up, and she was doing a pretty good job too. Then she started biting into his neck, but her dentures kept falling out.

"What have you done with all my witches? You crazy freak!" she shouted.

Leon had now fully turned into a werewolf, and he was loco-crazy, brimming with wolf-rage. He'd been angry at Roaring Meg his whole life, so this was a perfect opportunity to let rip, but deep down, Leon remembered Sasha's instructions, he wanted Meg alive, bummer.

Meg gripped her horrible hands around Leon's neck and tried her very best to strangle him. She squeezed him with all her strength, but this had very little effect on Leon –he was too strong.

Without any hesitation, Leon sunk his teeth deep into Meg's left arm. He took the biggest, juiciest bite he could manage. His sharp fangs ripped out a big piece of green lumpy witch flesh, Leon spat it out into the sky and went straight in for a second bite.

"Mmmmm... Witch blood, my favourite," he shouted.

Meg's ruby red ragu blood spilled out from her veins like thick tomato soup, then her black surfboard suddenly came whizzing by and hovered alongside the both of them. She was now in a lot of pain and had second thoughts about what she was doing. Leon's potent wolf-rage was terribly powerful and extremely offensive, so Meg jumped back on her board and decided to attack the ice cream van instead, but Leon was having none of that. He jumped on the board with Meg and continued fighting her. This really freaked me out because I was suddenly left sitting all alone in the motorbike sidecar with nobody driving. Leon and Meg beat the hell out of each other on that black surfboard. They behaved like a couple of sky surfing street fighters, while I slipped into a kamikaze nosedive. I had to act fast, but I couldn't open the side door. Mayday, I was going down. I kept bashing against the door again and again, then Max came along and opened it for me, yes! What a hero.

I climbed over to the driver's seat and quickly grabbed a hold of the handlebars. Penelope Jones flew alongside me. She didn't touch anything, but she gave me lots of encouragement; it was terribly windy. I had to turn this nosedive around quick-time. I was falling fast, getting closer and closer to the ocean below. I leaned forward, then I tried to pull up, and after maybe sixty seconds, I slowly levelled things out and gained some control, it was a damn close one, the tyres of IRON JOHN actually skimmed over the ocean, kissing the sea surface a few times, then I flew back up into the sky, phew-wee.

Max and Penelope stayed with me after that. I looked up high and saw that Leon and Meg were still at it, fighting their hearts out, then I looked up higher and saw the whole gang come shooting out from the ice cream van. They flew down to help Leon; it was a spectacular sight to see.

Betty stashed all her spare jet-powered rocket boards inside the van when we picked up all the witches from the laundrette – nice move, Betty. Everybody flew out on their own board – Sasha, Kelly Ann, Tigerlips, Betty, and three of The Fuzz Cats.

Fuzz Cat George stayed on board and continued flying the van. The whole gang steamed into Meg and tied her up with rope. She was completely outnumbered. Teamwork baby! They took her back up to the ice cream van and tied her to the passenger seat.

Leon was still pumped with anger and adrenaline. He wanted to carry on fighting Meg; he was so revved up. He wanted to rip her head off, but he somehow managed to control his wolf-rage. He stayed on Meg's black surfboard and kept well away from the ice cream van.

Back in the van, The Fuzz Cats quickly teamed up and gave Meg a hurricane-smacking-soul-whacking-triple-powered-hug-zap! But it had no effect on her; she was too strong. They tried ten more zaps, but it was a complete waste of time – they only tickled Meg. Then Sasha zapped Meg with a fierce paralysis spell. This spell held Meg inside a large frozen block of ice, and for a moment, she became motionless, but that only lasted ten seconds. Meg melted the ice with her fiery red eyes.

Sasha quickly tried another spell, zapping Meg with some purple magic. She instantly became tied up in a huge bundle of thick ropes, but her anger turned all the ropes into flames. Sweet heavens above, Meg was becoming a real stinker of a problem.

Then, Kelly Ann suddenly made her move. She acted fast as she pointed her new magic wand straight at Meg's head. Not really knowing what she was doing, Kelly Ann zapped some untamed magic right into Meg's face. This was the first time she used the magic wand, and the spell she threw turned out to be a real corker. She imagined a picture of Meg locked up inside a small cage made of thick solid steel, and the magic wand instantly honoured Kelly Ann's vision, awesome!

At last, we finally had Meg caged up and under our control. We all kept our fingers crossed and hoped that she wouldn't break free. I was just about coping on the flying motorbike. Max and Penelope never left my side, they truly were a couple of sweet genuine buddies.

We finally had ALL the witches in our possession. Yes!

CHAPTER 24
A TIGERY ACT OF KINDNESS

Hallelujah, we finally arrived at Hudson Bay. It was extremely windy and absolutely freezing, but that was nothing compared to what was coming. Leon continued gliding on Meg's black surfboard while I bobbed up and down on his motorbike, I was just about managing to keep control. Leon's passions were sky-high. The werewolf side of him wanted to rip Meg's face off. I remember how cool he looked standing on that surfboard; he stood like a legend as he howled majestically up to the sky. Steam came out of his mouth. I wasn't sure if he was howling at the moon or at Meg.

Then I looked up at the ice cream van and saw Tigerlips jump out with no parachute.

Like a fearless Tomcat, he glided through the sky and swiftly landed on the back of Meg's surfboard, almost knocking his brother off. Tigerlips quickly wrapped his arms around Leon and ordered him to fly down to the ocean. Leon did what he was told but deep down inside, he wanted to give Tigerlips a good punch on the nose – Leon's blood was hotter than lava.

"Come on! Hurry up, you crazy old wolf. Fly me

down lower."

Leon wanted to swipe Tigerlips right across the face for being so bossy, but instead, he did exactly what Tigerlips asked. This was 'DISCIPLINED-TEAMWORK-SPIRIT' in motion. This was a lesson for me, Leon showed me that teamwork is more important than any stubborn ego, no matter how strong the individual is.

They both flew down into the bay, and Tigerlips spontaneously dived into the ocean. As soon as he hit the water, he immediately started making lots of weird catty growling sounds. He did this just under the surface. I couldn't figure out what he was doing at first, but I soon realised he was sending out warning messages to all the sealife in the bay. Being one-third stingray and one-third electric eel, Tigerlips found it quite easy to communicate with all the creatures in the ocean.

He roared ferociously on a high aqua frequency level. He was basically telling everyone to clear off.

"It's evacuation time, so get out of the bay area, and stay away for twenty-four hours," this was the message he roared out.

Something very heavy was about to go down, then I saw the Titanic shipwreck up ahead. We were so close now. I'm pleased to say that the circus sack was still holding strong – we didn't lose a single witch. The final stages of Sasha's magnificent master plan were upon us.

CHAPTER 25
ONE BADASS SPELL

All the sealife had now swum out to the North Atlantic Ocean. They heard the warning voice from Tigerlips and quickly scooted away.

The ice cream van hovered steadily about fifty metres above the Titanic shipwreck; this was exactly what Sasha wanted. He grabbed a hold of the steel cage and flew Meg down on a jet-powered rocket board. Kelly Ann followed on another jet board. In one hand, she held her magic wand, and in the other, she held the suitcase filled with all the purple magic.

The Titanic shipwreck was barely visible. It was still underwater apart from one of the big chimney funnels, peek-a-booing just above sea level. Sasha gently took the magic wand from Kelly Ann and raised the Titanic up to the surface, allowing them to land on deck.

What happened next was extremely crazy – a very strange thing to witness indeed – and easily the best spell I ever saw. As soon as they landed on deck, Sasha pointed the wand up to the sky and got busy casting his last spell ever. Now I know this sounds a bit nuts, but this is what happened.

Sasha's fantastic Titanic spell attracted and manipulated all the thunderstorms from all over the world. He gathered all the electric thunder and lightning and somehow held it up in the sky, just above Hudson Bay.

There were crackles of angry lightning and rumbles of huge thunder that made the heavens shake, and a great deal of rainfall too. Sasha then added another component to the mix – he manipulated all the Northern Lights from Alaska and Norway. For some reason, they call these lights the Aurora Borealis; a mixture of beautiful green lights that dance graciously in the cold, dark wintry skies – they are wonderfully pretty. Well, Sasha sucked them over to the skies above Hudson Bay as well.

Sasha's spell was huge, maybe the biggest spell ever conducted by a wizard. Fire and ice mixed with electric sparks came pouring out from the magic wand and rushed up to the sky above, quickly reshaping the northern lights, along with all the wild untamed weather up there, the raw magic turned all the weather into a huge green electric horseshoe. Sasha looked like he was in a trance as he entwined all these elements together. He used sheer wizardry skill – the huge horseshoe glowed beautifully. It looked like the spell was working, but there was still a lot to do. Sasha's concentration was deep and serious; things were getting very tense now. In all honesty, I still didn't have a clue what he was up to.

He waved his arms all over the place, like a crazy conductor in front of a large orchestra, then he suddenly threw the wand up in the air and caught it with his other hand. He was showing off now, then the Titanic shipwreck started to wobble and vibrate – that was when Sasha gave the signal up to the ice cream van. It was time for Betty and The Fuzz Cats to come out and release all the green yukky witches. They slowly climbed down the tight ropes of the circus sack and waited for Sasha to give them the go-ahead.

Fuzz Cat George flew lower now; he positioned the circus sack to hover just two metres above the Titanic.

Sasha winked twice while pointing his free hand to the circus sack – this was his way of telling Betty and the three fuzzies to go-ahead with the unloading. They carefully opened the huge sack and gently poured all the witches out onto the open deck.

After five minutes of pouring, the sack was completely empty. All the witches were now resting on the Titanic, sitting on deck in a humongous green pile, and they were still sleeping, thank goodness. Betty and The three Fuzz Cats stayed close to Kelly Ann now, they all kept still on deck, as they watched Sasha do his thing.

Sasha then refocused all his attention back onto the green electric horseshoe above. I couldn't understand what he was doing, but I knew I could trust him. The horseshoe shined like bright emerald stones; it was the exact same shade as Betty's green eyes. Sparks jumped off it as it snapped and popped with electric power, then it suddenly began to expand and stretch out – it grew rapidly.

The Fuzz Cats loved the electric horseshoe because it made them glow up like fireflies. Leon watched the whole thing, as he stood on Meg's black surfboard, then he suddenly saw Tigerlip's head pop up from the ocean's surface, so he quickly flew down and picked his brother up. Tigerlips glowed like a firefly too; they both hurried over to the Titanic and landed on deck.

The horseshoe was massive now. It filled the whole of the Hudson Bay area, it was now time to move it into position.

Kelly Ann took a look over to the witches and saw

that some of them were beginning to wake up, she quickly told Sasha and he blasted a quick flash of the wand over to the pile, and they all fell back to sleep.

Sasha then lowered the huge green horseshoe down just enough for it to dip into the ocean. What was he doing?

I was still flying about on Leon's motorbike, watching the whole thing from above. Penelope was in the sidecar now, and Max held on tight to my shoulder. We decided to fly down and join the gang; I wanted to be close to Sasha.

All the gang were together now, apart from Fuzz Cat George – he was still at the wheel of the ice cream van, skilfully hovering above us.

I looked over to the huge pile of witches and saw that some of them were waking up again, Mamma Mia. That was the exact same moment when Sasha started barking loud orders at us. It was difficult to hear him because his voice was being flooded out by the sound of the hard-falling rain.

Sasha shouted over to Kelly Ann, "Kelly Ann, my love, I need you to open the suitcase now. Get the purple magic ready – hurry up, my darling."

None of us realised this at the time, but the whole shipwreck was now floating above sea level. It was completely out of the water and still rising. Sasha ordered Kelly Ann to leave all the purple magic right beside the humongous pile of witches.

"Ok, guys!" said Sasha. "You all have to get out of here now. We have a visitor coming, and if you want to stay alive, you need to get far away!" Everybody looked a bit confused; we didn't fully understand what Sasha meant. Who was visiting?

"Come on! Go! Go! There's no time to explain! You guys need to get out of here, now!" Sasha shouted like a crazy American wrestler, then he suddenly became very emotional. "Kelly Ann, Betty, I love you two angels with all my heart, but you guys really need to leave now, ok." Then Penelope Jones suddenly spoke up.

"You know guys, I think now would be a great time to get a quick group photo."

"Yes, let's do that!" Said Betty. She'd already taken out her phone and selfie stick. Sasha shouted one more time, he was under so much pressure now.

"If you're going to take a group picture just hurry up and do it now, make it snappy, ok."

So, we all quickly gathered around Sasha while he held his wand up to the sky, it had a huge stream of magic blasting out from it, it looked like a craggy moonbeam. We all smiled as we huddled and cuddled around him.

It's funny looking back. I always laugh to myself when I look at that picture because Roaring Meg is in the corner of the frame peering out from the steel cage, and it looks like she's trying to crack a little smile, bless her. Maybe deep down inside she wanted to be a part of the gang?

Betty took a couple of snaps and that was it. Job done, then I immediately picked up a feeling of 'Goodbye' in the air. I felt it in my rib, and when Kelly Ann and Betty gave their dad a quick hug goodbye, I knew something was up.

Sasha then released Meg from the steel cage and grabbed a hold of her; he had her fixed and locked under his left arm. He squeezed her with all his might, while his right hand continued conducting the mighty electric spell with the magic wand.

Following Sasha's orders we all started to get well away from the shipwreck. Betty and Kelly Ann both flew up to the ice cream van on a jet-powered rocket board. I flew on Meg's black surfboard; Penelope and Max flew alone. The three Fuzz Cats quickly climbed back up the circus ropes, and Leon and Tigerlips flew off on Leon's IRON JOHN motorbike. The only ones left on the Titanic now were Sasha, Meg, and all the sleeping witches.

The glow of the purple magic in the old leather suitcase suddenly doubled in strength; it just kept getting brighter and brighter. Remember, there was lots of purple magic inside the ship's steel frame and body as well, the whole shipwreck started to glow up. Everything was happening harmoniously, just the way Sasha planned it.

He started pointing his wand up to the sky with more passion now, and more magic stirred in the atmosphere – it was extremely powerful. Suddenly, lots of jagged bolts of purple lightning came spitting out of the magic wand. It was beautiful, and it created an abundance of energy around the whole bay. It turned the green horseshoe into a purple horseshoe, and it also made my rib glow.

I jumped back into the ice cream van with Betty and Kelly Ann, then I helped The Fuzz Cats climb back into the van as well, along with Max and Penelope. It was crazy windy up there.

Then I saw a box of sunglasses in the van, with a small note from Sasha: 'PUT THESE ON... QUICKLY NOW!' So, we all put our shades on and flew further away from the Titanic. On the back of the note was a scribbly message 'ICE LOLLIES FOR EVERYONE, TAKE A LOOK IN THE SMALL FRIDGE FREEZER, UNDER THE GLOVE COMPARTMENT'. I looked and found seven 'Fab' ice lollies, yummy, nice one Sasha!

The empty circus sack dangled below us. We had to stick to our promise and return it back to the circus people in Regents Park, but not yet – we were in the middle of something unique, and I didn't want to miss a thing. Looking out the side window, I saw Leon and Tigerlips hovering close by.

None of us knew what was going to happen next.

Sasha was a very mysterious man, he always kept us guessing. We were now in a safe place, far away enough to watch the completion of this fantastic spell. The wand waved back and forth in Sasha's right hand like he was writing poetry on an invisible blackboard; this made the massive electrical horseshoe slowly lower itself further down into the ocean.

All the electrical energy bubbled and fizzed as it dipped into the sea; electrical currents flowed in the water. It was a good thing Tigerlips got all the sealife to swim away – they would have been electrocuted to death, frizzle-fried for sure.

The Titanic shipwreck lifted itself even higher now, allowing enough space for the beautiful, electric horseshoe to scoop itself underneath.

At first, the Titanic nearly toppled over, but it soon locked itself into a perfectly set position. It was now sitting comfortably at the very bottom of the purple horseshoe; this was indeed a very rare sight to see.

Meg suddenly started to put up a bit of a fight with her old nemesis. She still wanted to kill Sasha, but that was impossible now. He was too empowered by all the magical energy oozing out from the wand and horseshoe. Nothing could stop him now. Sasha then made a loud noise that sounded like a huge lion's roar. He spontaneously shouted out two words: "WAKE UP!" It echoed all around the bay.

Even though I was a fair distance away, this still made

all the hairs on my arms stand on end. All the witches woke up in an instance.

Along with the whole gang (now wearing sunglasses) we continued watching, wondering what might happen next. Sasha suddenly threw the wand out from behind him like a boomerang, it flew across the ocean over to where The Paradox Twins were hovering. Leon reached out and caught it, he swiftly snatched it out of the air, cool move Leon, then he quickly placed it inside his leather jacket.

We all turned our heads back to the Titanic and saw how Sasha was now hugging Meg with all the wizard love he could muster. Every single witch was wide awake now, they quickly ran over to Sasha and steamed into him, their hearts were full of rage, anger and revenge. It looked like a riot was kicking off, but it didn't really matter. All that mattered was Sasha had to stay close to Meg and all the witches; the biggest surprise was still yet to come.

Sasha wouldn't let go of Meg, that was for sure. All I could see now was a big bundle of green bodies moving about, with Sasha and Meg hidden deep underneath. I think I saw Sasha's feet sticking out, I wasn't sure. His feet were pretty big. The witches made horrible noises, even though we were far away. I could still hear them moan; they whined like old pussycats yearning for milk.

It was an atrocious sight. The pile of stinky witches

grew higher and higher. Sasha and Meg were completely out of sight now, buried deep under a pile of green grotty stinkers.

Then I saw some movement come from the old brown leather suitcase – the purple magic suddenly came to life. It moved about like a ghost, like a cloud of purple mist, it then positioned itself right in the middle of the big pile of rioting witches.

I would never have guessed what was going to happen next, so I just sat back and watched-on while I bit into my fab ice lolly. I wish those fab lollies had more chocolate on them.

Far away in the distance, high up in the sky, something approached the bay. As it got closer, I saw how the horseshoe grew bigger and bigger. Everything was ready; everything was in position. It was a good thing I wore my sunglasses because the brightness was insane.

As fast as a bullet, an unidentified object came flying down towards us.

"Look!" shouted Betty. "It's Halley's comet!"

It shot straight past us!

Oh, my goodness, I was awestruck. I watched Halley's Comet fly down into the bay like a glittery bomb; it was awfully fast. It zoomed down towards the Titanic and automatically slotted itself into one side of the purple horseshoe.

This is what it did: IT SWOOPED IN, SWISHED

AROUND, AND ZOOMED STRAIGHT BACK UP IN TO THE SKY, ALL IN LESS THAN HALF A SECOND! AND IT TOOK EVERYTHING WITH IT!

It took Sasha, Meg, all the witches, the old Titanic shipwreck, and ALL the purple magic – everything got catapulted back up into the sky. It was the fastest U-turn in history and the coolest rescue ever.

At the exact moment of the rescue, Sasha instructed all the purple magic to turn himself and Meg (along with all the mini witches) back into shooting stars!

Halley's Comet simply gave them the big 'kick-start' they needed. But this time, just by sheer chance, Meg, Sasha and all the mini witches melded into one big shooting star! They looked like a space rocket going back up to the top of the sky – a big silver firework destined to race and shine across the universe, forever!

I watched the whole thing with the gang; thank goodness we had our dark glasses on. There was even a little pair of mini shades for Max to wear. We all gazed on and marvelled at the amazing sight through the van's windscreen – it was astonishing. Max and Penelope were speechless. I think Max was a bit sad to see Sasha go.

Just below us, Leon and Tigerlips watched the spectacular transformation as well. They protected their eyes with tinted motorcycle goggles. We were all so very impressed with the grand finale of Sasha's unorthodox master plan; it was a huge success, what a hero!

That was the last time we ever saw Sasha, or Meg. It turned out to be a very historic and triumphant day: the day two old shooting stars got turned back into one brand new shooting star. Sonic Sasha and Roaring Meg finally made it back home, all done with a little bit of help from Halley's comet.

As soon as they reached the top of the sky, they quickly disappeared, then the horseshoe disappeared, and all the thunder and lightning and rain drifted back to other parts of the world. All the clouds and pretty Northern Lights drifted off too, and we suddenly found ourselves in the middle of a beautiful blue sky day.

Penelope spoke up, "Well, I must say, that was the second coolest thing I have ever seen!"

"Really?" I asked.

"So what's the coolest thing you've even seen, Penelope?"

"Rocky One, of course! I love a good boxing movie."

Penelope was crackers down to the bone, but I loved her, I had grown to love every single member of the gang.

We decided to land in a nearby Canadian forest; we set the van down in Wapusk National Park. We were all feeling overwhelmed with emotion and adrenalin. We needed something to help us relax, so we decided to make some green tea and have a little picnic.

CHAPTER 26
THE EXPLODING DIAMOND
EXPRESS

He'd only been gone for ten minutes, but we were all missing Sasha like crazy. It was brilliant that he got back to where he truly belonged, and it was terrific that Meg got saved from all her dark evil ways. Deep down inside this made us very happy, but our leader was gone, and that sucked! Sasha was our father, our captain, our father-figure – a real heavy feeling of grief ran through the whole gang. It felt like we were at a funeral.

Kelly Ann and Betty cried so much, and when I saw them cry, it made me cry. The Fuzz Cats and The Paradox Twins looked awfully sad as well.

Max Redwood perched himself on my shoulder, while Penelope sat on Leon's motorbike. She was in a right state, sobbing like a little child. She really loves Sasha – we all do.

Nobody knew that Sasha was going to perform such a unique and mystifying spell; he kept the last stage of the master plan all to himself. It made me smile knowing he was free again, but we never knew we were going to miss him so much, and we never really got to say goodbye, oh well.

Suddenly, without any warning, my mood changed. I started to feel a bit lighter in my heart. This was all triggered off by a tickling sensation in my magic rib. It moved around, under my T-shirt; it does that sometimes.

It was trying to tell me something. I can't explain the feeling, but Sasha's rib intuitively told me that there was something important in the back pocket of Betty's jeans.

As the gang sobbed away, I spoke up and asked Betty to check her back pocket. She was so upset; her beautiful green eyes were drenched with tears. She checked her jeans and slowly pulled out a perfectly folded piece of paper. As she opened it, her face lit up.

"It's a letter from Dad," she said. The sniffles stopped and everyone became silent. "Ok, I'm going to read it out." We all waited, with a new feeling of excitement in our hearts.

"Dear Gang,

Hi Guys, Sasha here. I just wanted to congratulate you all, and let you know that I love you. I'm so proud of you guys. You all came together and worked like a fantastic dream-team. My goodness, you guys are the best! Thank you so much for your commitment to our mission. I feel so privileged to have been a part of this fantastic tenacious gang.

I've got you all deep in my heart, now and forever, and for the record, I want you to know that I would love to fly down and say bon voyage and thank you in person, but as you have probably already guessed, I'm not a wizard anymore. I have gone back to being a shooting star, and unfortunately, I won't be able to just pop in and say hi. I'm too big and powerful for that. I've got to stay up here in space now – this is my home. This is where I belong.

There is something I want you guys to know. I will always be connected to all of you, so whenever you guys are feeling happy, and your heart is filled with joy and love, I will feel it too. I may be millions of miles away, but I still feel all the feelings you guys feel – your joy, your sadness, your happiness. I feel all of it, so always remember that when you're feeling happy, it makes me shine just that little bit stronger. It makes me fly and race faster, and this helps me become a more magnificent shooting star. The same thing goes for anyone reading these words, anybody who chooses to feel good on planet Earth makes me shine stronger. So please promise me that you'll always try to stay positive and shine strong down there on planet Earth. It's a beautiful planet.

Earth is a lovely place. Don't ever be afraid to shine and laugh and make jokes and have fun and dance and giggle. Life is short guys – you don't want to end up like Roaring Meg, keeping all that anger and resentment in your heart. It's a crime living that way. You guys are above all that crap – you must never forget this. You can always rise above anger and fear and dark energy.

I want to give my Italian coffee bar to The Paradox Twins. I think you guys will be happy there. Just try not to scare all the customers away. Tell them you like dressing up for Halloween every day of the year, and make sure you look after Max. Give him seeds and fresh bread every day. As far as I'm concerned, this tenacious gang is still a fantastic gang. I don't want you guys to break up.

I want you guys to promise me that you won't waste your lives watching rubbish television, and spending too much time on your phones.

Don't waste time playing computer games, read some books or learn to play a musical instrument instead, learn to enjoy life. Earth is a beautiful and glorious planet, enjoy it, protect it, and spread love. Don't let yourselves become brainwashed by the dark energy that Meg accidentally created – be like Sonic Sasha, focus on light energy instead.

Meg forgot who she was, she lost track of her real identity, that's all. She was lost and sad, depressed, angry and greedy. This made her want to make other people lost and sad and depressed. She became a sick control-freak, but that's all over now. She's my co-pilot now, riding shotgun with me through space, she's happy again, yeah baby!

I want all you guys to be a good example of how fantastic it is to be a little bit weird, a little bit different. Always be who you really are. It's cool to be a little bit eccentric – embrace it.

I would now like to tell Kelly Ann and Betty that I am so proud of the both of you. I love you both, so much! Your mother, Jennie, is a mermaid, and she lives deep in the ocean. I'm sure Tigerlips can help you find her.

I would like the both of you to try and reconnect with your mother, really get to know her. She wants to see you guys again – it's been too long. She loves you so much.

You two girls never developed any mermaid fins or gills because my DNA is very strong. You took after me, more than you took after your mother, but there is one thing you all have in common – you're all gorgeous and beautiful!

Now I would like to tell you about my other rib. I left it stashed away in Highgate Cemetery. It's a gift for your mother. It has intelligent magic inside that's just waiting to make her happy again. This rib will allow her to transform herself into a woman any time she likes. She can be a mermaid or a woman – it's up to her. You can find my other magical rib in the exact same place you found Louise's rib. It's buried six feet deeper in the exact same spot. All Jennie needs to do is wear the rib around her neck at bedtime, and when she wakes up in the morning, the rib will be inside her. I would like you guys to give Jennie's wand back to her as well, I hope one day she will teach Kelly Ann how to use it. The wand has many deep powers and beautiful secrets.

I also want to express a huge hearty thanks to The Fuzz Cats. You guys are the coolest cats in the universe! Thanks for all your hard work and unbreakable commitment"

Betty took a break from reading the letter. There was more to read, but we all needed a little timeout to digest everything Sasha said.

Max Redwood was still perched on my shoulder, when he started whistling a tune. That was a good sign. He immediately took advice from Sasha's letter and became more cheerful in a matter of seconds.

I really liked having Max on my shoulder. It made me feel good that he chose to be close to me before anyone else in the gang; he was a cool robin. Betty was now ready to carry on reading the letter. Sasha was writing for me now.

"I now need to say something to Louise: I need to apologise to her for all the trouble I've put her through. I think Louise has been a brave little member of the gang. She's had a very tough time with the way things went for her, and it's time she knows the truth about her mother and father. I was there when they disappeared in the hot air balloon on that sunny afternoon. I was the guy on the beach offering the hot air balloon rides; that was me in disguise. I was the one who took your parents away, Louise, only for safekeeping; I was merely looking after them.

I am so sorry for putting you through all the tough stuff, but I had to do this. I knew how crazy Meg was. I knew she was going to hurt your mother and father to try and get to you. She was so messed up with greed and anger and rage and selfishness.

She knew nothing about kindness; she simply wanted to destroy and control everything. She would have been happy to kill your parents, get rid of them once and for all, but I would not allow this.

That's when I decided to take your parents far away and keep them out of Meg's reach. Louise, you'll be very glad to know that both your parents are alive and well – they live in the Hawaiian Islands.

They own a fantastic little restaurant on Ewa beach in Honolulu – it's called the Bamboo Boogie Burger Bar, and they're expecting you. They want you and the whole gang to drop by for burgers and milkshakes."

Betty stopped reading the letter for a moment, and we all looked at each other with excited eyes; my heart felt like singing. I asked Betty to read that part of the letter again, just to make sure I heard what I thought I heard. She read it out, and I began to cry. Holy smoking ping pong balls! I was suddenly overwhelmed with emotion.

"I could murder a burger and wash it down with a

milkshake – this picnic food sucks!" said Leon.

"Yes, I fancy a burger too," said Tigerlips.

Sasha's fantastic letter cheered everybody up. I suddenly felt happy, scared, excited, and nervous all at the same time – it was great.

I couldn't believe it. I was going to see my mum and dad again, yes!

"Is that the end of the letter?" I asked.

Betty looked down and said, "No, there's a little bit more."

This is what it said:

"Now listen guys, I want all of you to get back into the ice cream van, and Leon, you get back on your motorbike. I want you all to promise me that you'll go straight to Honolulu and have a big party, just for me.

Get yourselves over to the Bamboo Boogie Burger Bar, and have some fun. I want you guys to celebrate your magnificent achievements. We have all gotten rid of Meg's sick, selfish, dark side, and all the mini witches too. Now, that's a huge achievement! This is a perfect reason to have a great party.

Always remember, guys: TEAMWORK MAKES THE DREAMWORK! Now, get going."

That was the end of the letter, and everyone cheered out loud. We all felt so much better after hearing Sasha's wise, caring words.

Then, Penelope suddenly spoke up, "Come on, let's go. Everybody back in the ice cream van! Hurry, hurry!"

Everyone was excited. The Fuzz Cats glowed up like Christmas tree lights. My heart was overwhelmed with joy. We all climbed back into the van, and Leon stubbornly hopped back on his triumph motorbike. Before we took off, he made a quick announcement. He said he was happy to take the circus sack back to the travelling gypsies in Regent's Park. We all thanked him and helped tie the tent to the motorbike. Penelope decided to go with Leon; she stayed in the motorbike's little sidecar. She's the coolest ghost ever. They swiftly flew off to London while the rest of the gang flew to Honolulu.

As we made our way over to the Hawaiian Islands, the tenacious gang came up with a new name for Sasha and Meg's new shooting star.

We all decided to call it, 'The Exploding Diamond Express!'

CHAPTER 27
ALOHA

We soon arrived in hot, sunny Honolulu. It was like stepping into a postcard – palm trees and blue skies everywhere.

Fuzz Cat George landed the ice cream van on the flat sands of Ewa beach. I was so excited! I felt so good inside; I really thought my parents were gone for good. Betty put her arm around me and shared my joy. She felt like my big sister now.

I looked over yonder and saw a huge palm tree

standing tall in the sand. As I looked closer, I noticed there were two shops sitting under it.

The first shop was a beach shop, selling surfboards, wetsuits, T-shirts, beach towels, and stuff like that. The second shop was the Bamboo Boogie Burger Bar. Yes, that was it – we found it.

"Come on! Let's go grab a burger," said Tigerlips. Everyone, apart from myself, was hungry. I couldn't think about food; I had too many emotions dancing about inside. I had busy butterflies in my heart, happy thoughts in my head, and jumping jitterbugs in my tummy.

We got some strange looks from the local people as we walked along the beach. I guess it's not every day you see people like The Fuzz Cats and Tigerlips. Kelly Ann and Betty looked pretty cosmic too. I guess I looked a bit loopy with my blue hair and a little robin perched on my shoulder, but I didn't care.

Max Redwood was still singing and tweeting lovely music; he sang straight from his little heart.

I guess Leon and Penelope were probably in London by now. It was awful nice of them to take the circus tent back. They'd join us soon enough, no doubt about that.

We soon found ourselves outside the main door of the Bamboo Boogie Burger Bar. I took a deep breath and walked in. I immediately saw both my parents at the bar. Mum was cleaning the coffee machine while Dad mopped the floor. They had a small digital radio playing Hawaiian tunes in the background, and just by sheer luck, they were playing my favourite song in the whole world, a song called, "Somewhere Over the Rainbow," by Brother IZ.

"Louise! Is that you? Oh, my goodness!" shouted my dad. My heart flickered as it skipped a couple of beats.

"Louise! My lovely Louise!" Dad dropped his mop and came running over to me. He picked me up and hugged and squeezed me with all the love in his heart. He spun me around and around; I felt like the richest girl in the world. He cried like a big baby, and so did I.

Then my mum screamed and cried out with uncontrollable happiness, "Louise!"

She hopped over the bar and accidentally put her foot in the bucket my dad was using, then she tripped over the mop and fell flat on her face – my goodness she was so excited. She quickly bounced back up on her feet and ran over to us, throwing both her arms over me and Dad. We were a happy family again, yes!

My goodness, I had so much to tell them. I introduced Mum and Dad to the whole gang. Everybody was so happy to meet my parents; it was a lovely occasion.

"I'll have one of your finest Bamboo Burgers, please, sir," said Tigerlips to my dad.

"Yes, of course," he said. "Bamboo Burgers for

everyone." As soon as all the introductions were finished, Dad went straight to the kitchen and cooked up a storm of burgers, and Mum made over a dozen yummy milkshakes and smoothies, and a coffee for Betty, of course – she loves her black coffee. We had so many different flavour shakes to choose from: coconut, strawberry, raspberry, caramel, chocolate, banana, vanilla. They were delicious. Everyone raised a glass, and we all made a toast to Sonic Sasha.

Just as we finished our burgers and shakes, a man walked into the restaurant and spoke to my mum. He was a delivery guy, and he had something special for us in his truck outside. It was something quite fantastic.

My mum signed the delivery papers, and the man walked back out to fetch our present. He soon came back with a huge American jukebox. He rolled it in on a big old trolley; it was so cool. It was a classic rock 'n' roll one. The guy placed it in the corner of the restaurant by the little dance floor. The Fuzz Cats helped him move it into position; they were good at removal work.

It was a genuine vintage Wurlitzer jukebox that played real vinyl records. It was an absolute beauty.

I suddenly noticed a little note attached to it. The note said, 'Dance your blues away! Love from Sasha x'.

Ha! That was all the note said, so we plugged it in and played lots of great music for hours and hours – party time had arrived.

The Bamboo Boogie Burger Bar was the right place

to be for a good boogie, and the burgers were so tasty. We danced to rock n roll music like crazy fools until the sun went down.

Juke Box from the Bamboo Boogie Burger Bar

Then Leon and Penelope suddenly arrived. Leon filled his belly up with burgers and milkshakes in no time, and soon after that, he and Penelope joined in with all the silly dancing.

I was laughing so much at the way Leon danced; he was a lovely character when he opened-up. The Fuzz Cats had some funny dance moves too – they were breakdancing. Tigerlips and Kelly Ann were inseparable – they danced together for hours. Betty was having a lot of fun dancing with The Fuzz Cats, she did the Tango with Fuzz Cat Sam, and Max Redwood stayed on my shoulder the whole night long. He was my new best friend.

There was a happy silly song on the jukebox called 'Bamboo'. It was very stupid and funny, we played it over and over.

Penelope danced on the bar like a drunk, happy monkey, while Leon did the Pachanga with my mum – that was a funny sight to see. We were all having a magnificent time.

The loud music coming from the Bamboo Boogie Burger Bar attracted many of the local people from the beach. More and more people kept coming in as the music played throughout the evening. It was the happiest day of my life! I was reunited with my mum and dad, and I now had a whole new bunch of fantastic friends: the magnificent tenacious gang. They were more like family to be honest – I felt truly blessed.

Suddenly, Fuzz Cat George came up to me and gave me a little gift. It was the original lullaby music box from the ice cream van.

The music box from the Fuzz Cat's ice cream van

"Here you go, Louise," he said.

"This is a small gift from The Fuzz Cats. If you should ever need us, just play this music box, and we'll come running straight to your aid."

George suddenly turned around and acted out some crazy dance moves. He wiggled his bum as he walked back to the dance floor; he made me chuckle. It was a lovely gift.

I needed to take a break because I was feeling quite overwhelmed with all the good stuff going on, so I went outside to get some air. I walked out onto the beach and took some deep breaths. The setting sun was just slipping out of sight, and the cool night air felt lovely. I saw that my dad had set up a beautiful barbecue on the beach, not too far from the restaurant. He cooked for everyone.

"Free Burgers! Free Kebabs! Come and get it folks!" he shouted. He was busy for hours.

I decided to walk further out along the beach for a while. I needed to digest everything in my heart and soul. All this good stuff was quite a shock to my system you know, a nice shock but still a shock nonetheless. As I walked along the sand, I looked up to the sky and saw the moon and all the stars shining down. I had so much to be grateful for. I felt so glad to be alive.

I suddenly felt a deep, powerful warmth come up from inside me; it was my rib, glowing up again. It felt so positive and strong. I turned and looked at Max on my left shoulder, and he whistled a few happy notes to me, then I suddenly noticed something up in the sky.

It was Sonic Sasha and Roaring Meg whizzing by on the Exploding Diamond Express. I couldn't help myself – I started to cry. I had so much love for Sasha. As they swished over the Hawaiian Islands, they left a sparkly message in the sky, written in stardust it said, "KEEP SHINING, LOUISE!"

I smiled and blew a kiss up to them, then I went back into the Bamboo Boogie Burger Bar and danced the whole night away with my friends and family. Max never left my shoulder; in fact, he's still sitting on my shoulder today.

I found it hard to explain my adventures to new friends and other people, so I decided to put my story into a book. The book that you've just finished reading. Thank you so much for reading my story.

Until the next time, this is Louise Buttersky saying goodbye and ...

KEEP SHINING!
THE END

See ya!

Louise x

Louise
and the
Laundrette Lady

Written by Tony Andrews

Hi. This is Tony Andrews. I just wanted to say thanks for reading LOUISE AND THE LAUNDRETTE LADY.

Always remember that the best things in life are LOVE and KINDNESS – that's it. It's that simple. I hope to meet you one day and give you a big high five!

Bye for now.

Tony x